BILLIONAIRE'S OBSESSION

MAGICAL MATCHMAKER BOOK 2

AMANDA ADAMS

ABOUT: BILLIONAIRE'S OBSESSION

I have three rules I live by when building multi-billion-dollar companies. Rule number one: don't sleep with your employees. Rule number two: never, ever, ever sleep with your employees. And Rule number three: listen idiot, she's obviously gorgeous but you can't have her.

Only now… she quit… or she's leaving… or, whatever. I've had my eyes on her for two years. I practically get in my ten thousand steps each day just by making excuses to walk by her desk…catch a glimpse.

And now I seem to have contracted a serious case of *coitus interruptus*.

Love in an elevator… not so fast. Hot and sweaty yet unfulfilled… you're suffering from the side effects of coitus interruptus.

Sex on the beach… sounds yummy. You might think so, but sand in the nether regions can be just another side effect of coitus interruptus when an ever-so-nice family decides to stroll down the beach at the perfect time.

And the woman I'm losing sleep over? I actually think she is enjoying my misery.

I won't stop now. And if that means I need a little help from a mysterious friend playing matchmaker? I won's say no. I'm desperate. Love is a trickster, but I've faced fiercer enemies and emerged victorious. I must have her.

Billionaire's Obsession
Copyright © 2019 by Amanda Adams
ISBN: 978-1-7959-0104-8

All Rights Reserved. No part of this book may be reproduced or transmitted in any form or by any means, electrical, digital or mechanical including but not limited to photocopying, recording, scanning or by any type of data storage and retrieval system without express, written permission from the author.

Published by Amanda Adams

Adams, Amanda
Billionaire's Obsession

Cover design copyright 2019 by Tydbyts Media

CHAPTER 1

*L*indsey

IT'S one thing to be in Vegas for a weekend romp with the girls and a whole other thing to be in Vegas on the job. If I had to select my current relationship status with Sin City, I'd toggle between love and hate, hour-by-hour, hell minute-by-minute. While I linger in my hotel suite, gathering my toiletries and folding clothes, my mind wanders from another week of massaging and manipulating chaos to something else.

What I could be doing.

What I should be doing.

I should be sitting on the edge of my bed, a gorgeous and naked man gazing adoringly up at me, while I smoke a cigarette, exhausted and delightfully sore in all the right places, yet sated and triumphant. Who cares that I don't even smoke... that's not the damn point. If it meant I could have a hot lover in bed next to me, I would definitely light one up.

Instead, my companion in bed is an open suitcase.

I do love working for a company full of young, intelligent people, but why Vegas? Why? For the love of hedonism... why? And on New Year's weekend... again.

But I don't need to ask why. Gambling, free drinks, amazing restaurants, shows and the all-important, unending parade of attractive single people who leave their inhibitions at home. Every programmer and engineer who works for Michael, no matter how nerdy, becomes a heck of a lot more attractive when they let slip that their boss has been very generous with stock options in a company about to go public. Most will be twenty something millionaires within six months.

My pitiful amount of options pale in comparison; such is the life of a corporate event coordinator. Undercompensated and underappreciated.

Underappreciated until the hotel staff fails to set up a meeting room, A/V doesn't work or a hungover employee pukes in the hallway. Then it's Lindsey to the rescue, and she's the greatest thing since, well... since the last time she saved your ass.

But I do love the work. Organizing massive events, managing complex schedules, coordinating travel for hundreds and hard-core negotiations with hotels all give me a tremendous amount of satisfaction. Event week is my time to shine, to take charge and run the show.

The problem is I'm not in charge, not of my life and not of my career, and the time has come to change. A bachelor's degree from Cornell and an MBA from Northwestern were not meant to lead to a, more or less, dead end job. I've worked too damn hard, and it's time to make a change.

Back to the bathroom for one last scan, to make sure I haven't forgotten anything, my plan is to have everything ready for the morning, so I can just get up and go. As I turn, my phone lights up and buzzes across the end table. I can see that it's my kiss ass assistant Chad… again. I hesitate to answer, but if I don't, he'll keep calling. And keep calling. Why can't he do anything without asking for permission first?

"Hi, Chad."

"Hey, Lindsey, sorry to bother you again but there's this guy down here who works for the hotel; he says we can't set up our own A/V, he has to do it."

"Tell him he is full of shit, it's in our contract. We take care of our own A/V."

"I tried to tell him, but he's not listening. He insists and says it's union rules."

Fucking Las Vegas unions. You can't even wipe your own ass. You have to let one of their people do it for you so they can get their cut. "Chad, you have to be firm. It's our last event of the weekend, and it's for fucking karaoke. Why is he bothering us now? Tell him to check with the event manager." *The asshole thinks that if he jumps in now, he can charge us for every event.*

"No. Yes. No, well I did that, but he won't leave and he's huge. He's trying to take our equipment."

When Chad starts stuttering and repeating himself, it's time to interrupt and get him back on track. "Damn it, Chad. Fine, I'll be right down. Stall him and do not let him take anything." Hotels are notorious for killing you with A/V equipment and setup fees. Five hundred dollars for a microphone setup in a room and another five hundred to move that same microphone to another room, are you kidding me? It's cheaper to truck in our own equipment, so we do.

"Thanks, boss, please hurry."

"I will, Chad, and stop calling me boss."

"Right, sorry, boss, I mean Lindsey."

"Bye, Chad."

I can't help but shake my head and cover my face with my hands after ending my call with Chad. I'm sure he'll take over for me, and I suddenly feel bad for wanting to leave. He's bound to fuck everything up the first time he's in charge of an event. He's such a wuss. The first hotel he has to negotiate with is going to kill him.

I hang up and move my thumb over to shut down my phone's screen before I set it down, but out of the corner of my eye, I catch sight of an email notification.

My breath catches in my throat as my self-diagnosed, totally not real, but majorly severe case of email apnea kicks in. Whatever it is cannot be good, not when ninety-eight percent of the people I work with are not in the office but drunk and gyrating to horribly sung hits of the seventies, eighties and nineties.

Ah, but what could go wrong? It's Las Vegas, nothing ever goes wrong in this city. Right? Yeah... right.

I'm still holding my breath as the email fills my screen:

HEY, Lindsey! Hope all is well. Wanted to touch base with you regarding our spring break event this year. Are you still interested? I know you mentioned you were starting your own firm but had not heard anything further. We really need to make this year special and are planning a massive event, way larger than we can handle in-house. We need a pro and I mentioned your name to our CEO. Let me know if you are interested. I know it is a long holiday weekend, not sure if you are working but we are short on time and need to make a decision. We are also planning several other events this year so if all goes well... Let me know ASAP.

Thanks
Luke McKenna
VP of Operations, Excel Ventures, Inc.

. . .

OH MY GOD. Oh my god. Oh. My. God. Totally not what I was expecting, and I am so excited I can't stop pacing around my tiny hotel room. I've been putting out feelers for months, dreamt of starting my own event-planning firm for years, but never expected this. Excel Ventures would be a huge get. They are one of the largest and most successful venture capital firms in the area and the connections I could get... I want to scream I am so happy. This is it. With this one account I can start my own company and begin to build something for myself. It would mean quitting my job and risking every dollar I have ever saved but it could be everything I ever dreamed of.

I am in disbelief as I begin to type a reply:

Luke,

Thank you so much for thinking of me. I...

And an incoming text message interrupts. It's from Chad of course. *Please hurry, Lindsey, I need help.*

My Lord... what a pussy. The email will have to wait, and I begin my search for a pair of shoes. The only pair I haven't packed yet are the heels I wore to the cocktail party I just came from. *Shit.* They are rose red and gorgeous but not all that comfortable and it's a twenty minute walk back to the convention area. I'd rather put up with sore feet than unpack my whole suitcase, so I slip them on and head for the door; Lindsey to the rescue once again.

CHAPTER 2

Michael

THESE GUYS ARE hilarious and drunk but who cares, that's why we're here. Coders pop like a cork from a shaken champagne bottle if they don't take time to let loose and remember that they are real people. I've seen it before and learned my lesson. They plug in and the line between reality and virtual reality becomes almost indistinguishable. Sure these trips to Vegas are expensive but they are invaluable for retaining top talent and keeping them sane. I pay them a ton, and when we go public, they will all be rich, but they'll remember Jessica's horrible drunk singing long after the joy of buying a BMW has worn off.

"Michaelssssup?" Tyler Johnson leans on my

shoulder and tries to whisper in my ear but doesn't realize he is yelling. "We love you, man. Thanks fer doin' zis. You going t'sing?" Tyler is a brilliant system architect who will likely fall over if I move. The alcohol on his breath is almost enough to give me a contact drunk.

"No, I haven't had enough to drink for that."

"You want my drink?" He shoves his Bloody Mary in my face, nearly jamming the celery up my nose.

"No thanks, buddy." I push his drink back and he takes a long swig, which he finishes with a triumphant crunch on the celery top. "I don't think anyone wants to suffer through my singing again."

"C'mon, man. You can't be worse'n Jessica. D'ya hear her. I almost peed my pants."

"Yes, she was great, she fully commits."

"Yeah she does. She's awesome. I'ma go talk to her. See ya later, Michael."

"Bye, Tyler." I can't help but laugh at him as he stumbles toward Jessica's table. She is dancing on her chair and singing louder than the person on the microphone. Tyler stands beside her, smiling and staring for what feels like an eternity, then pulls up a chair, climbs on and joins in the singing. It's only a matter of time before he falls. I hope our insurance is paid up.

It's been a great weekend, but I can't take any more socializing and head toward the door to make my escape.

It's late and most people are in the party or at the

casino, so the walk back looks to be a lonely one. I could really use some fresh air, so I exit the long hallway and take the sidewalk back to the hotel. Three Long Island Ice Teas in one night is just enough to give me a mighty buzz, and I'm hoping the warm, dry night air will help clear my head. I always appreciate that our event coordinator Lindsey books us in an all-suite hotel separate from the casino. I prefer to keep the bright lights, constantly ringing slot machines, and smoky haze separate from where I sleep.

And speak of the devil. As I round the corner for the final stretch to the hotel lobby, there she is just ahead of me. I think about calling out to her but stop myself and enjoy the view instead. She is one sexy young woman and her ass in that skirt looks amazing as she walks ahead of me. If she didn't work for me, I would beg her for a date though I'd settle for a Vegas quickie. Several times at the office I felt sure she caught me staring at her, but she never let on if she noticed. She has the build of a former athlete and I love that; firm and ample rounded ass, strong muscular legs, slender torso and beautiful perky tits. I can only imagine what that ass feels like in that skirt as it flexes and flows with each stride.

Oh to be the fabric hugging that ass.

That should be my next startup… virtual reality that transfers that sensation directly to your brain. I'd make billions.

The fact that she is barefoot and carrying a pair of

red high heels in one hand and her leather planner in the other hand as she struts, completes the perfect picture. I wish the walk were ten miles longer.

As she nears the door to the hotel entrance, I jog up beside her. "Let me get that door for you."

"Where did you come from?" she asks.

"I was at the cocktail and karaoke party." Damn this woman is sexy. She always seems to have a pencil tucked behind her ear and it drives me crazy in a bookish kind of way. Hot and intelligent is a magical combination.

"Have you been behind me the whole walk back here? Why didn't you say anything?"

As I open the door and she enters ahead of me, I wish I could tell her the truth, but my dick is almost fully hard from watching her while contemplating my virtual reality idea and I'm afraid she'd notice. "No. Well yes, just since the last turn. I didn't want to disturb you." She squints her eyes at me and tilts her head, but I think she bought it.

"How was the party, did you sing?"

"Me? No. I just enjoy watching. Great event though, you did an amazing job organizing all this." We cross the lobby together and head to the bank of elevators. I'm not sure if it's the late night air or three stiff drinks but she looks more beautiful than ever.

"Oh, you like to watch huh?" She grins up at me as we join four other people waiting for an elevator to arrive. Did she just say what I think she said? Is she flirting with me? "Well, thanks. I'm glad everything went well. Everybody seemed to enjoy themselves."

The light above the left door illuminates and we follow the others as the doors open. Lindsey moves to the number panel, presses the number twenty and twenty-one. "I'm on twenty-one." I say.

"I know, I booked your room remember. I'm on twenty."

"Of course, thanks."

The elevator lurches upward and everybody assumes the usual elevator stance; phony smiles before facing forward, staring at the changing floor number, minimize the awkward conversation and pray nobody has bad body odor. Check, check, check and check. The only other lighted number on the panel is the tenth floor.

Six, Seven, Eight.

As we near the tenth floor, I catch a whiff and realize that I may have been a bit hasty with that final check. Thankfully, the pumped in perfumed air of the hotel overcomes in the battle for aromatic supremacy as the elevator dings and the other four passengers exit, leaving me alone with Lindsey.

She moves to my left as the doors close again, and I can't help but joke about our former elevator companions. "Phew, glad they're gone. I was starting to get a little worried."

"I was hoping that wasn't you." She waves her hand in front of her nose and grins.

"Oh nice. Thanks a lot." Eleven, twelve. "I thought it was you."

"Whatever, you jerk." She shoves me and I exaggerate her strength as I throw myself against the side of the elevator. Right as I impact the wall, the elevator jerks to a stop between the fifteenth and sixteenth floor and the lights go out.

"Ouch. See what you did." I move to the panel and push some buttons. "You broke it."

"You did it, you faker." She moves next to me, and I hear her pushing at the buttons also.

"What are you doing?"

"Maybe it's mad at you because you broke it." She pushes at my side and her red high heel shoes brush against my knee.

"You think your touch is more magical than mine?"

"I can promise you it is. What do you think is happening?"

I can't decide if she's flirting with me again. Twice within ten minutes when she is always one hundred percent business can't be my imagination. "I'm guessing the hotel lost power, and we're probably stuck in here together until it comes back on again." My cock is telling me I am not imagining her flirtation and rises to join the conversation.

"Which one is the emergency call button?" She leans forward, presses a button and the elevator plunges for what feels like an eternity. As it jerks to a stop again, Lindsey has fallen into me and we are facing each other, she is hugging my waist and pressing hard into me. I wrap my arms around her, and I know she can feel my stiffening cock pressing against her. "Stop breaking the elevator please." I feel ridiculous, but I pull her closer. We could plunge to our deaths at any moment, and all I can think about is fucking this gorgeous woman before I die.

"You think we'll die?" She's turned her face up to mine and her hot breath is at my mouth.

"We might," I say as I press my mouth onto hers and kiss her deeply. I hear her heels and her planner hit the floor behind me as she thrusts her tongue into mine.

CHAPTER 3

indsey

I HAVE no idea what has come over me and I don't care. I have had the hots for Michael since my first day on the job and now we're stuck in this damn elevator, likely to plunge to our deaths at any minute, and I just shoved my tongue down his throat. *Fuck it. What happens in Vegas...* He's never so much as looked my way more than once and now his cock is rock hard against my stomach, and I think I've soaked through my panties in record time.

I stop and pull back. "Are you sure about this?"

"No." He steps back, and I can hear him breathing hard. "I can't. You work for me. I never date anyone who works for me."

"I'm not asking you for a date." I step forward.

"You know what I mean. I can't"

"But I don't work for you anymore. Well... not exactly, almost."

"What? What do you mean you don't work for me anymore? Why haven't I heard anything about this?" He places his hand on my hip and holds me in place.

"I gave notice. I've decided to start my own business." So I am stretching the truth and jumping off a cliff at the same time. At this moment, stuck in this elevator with my crazy-sexy boss, for some strange reason, I don't seem to care. I step forward to close the gap between us and kiss him deeply again.

"Fuck it," he says. "What happens in Vegas—"

"Stays in Vegas." I finish his sentence. "You read my mind."

He spins us, places both hands on the bottom side of my ass and lifts me as he pushes my back against the wall of the elevator. I lift my left leg and wrap it around his hips and lower my waist to his to grind my engorged clit on his hard cock. He pauses kissing me and arches his head back. His voice growls, "You are so damn sexy." And his mouth is back on mine.

He moves his hand to the hem of my skirt and shoves the fabric up as he moves his right hand up my leg. As he nears the bottom of my ass, I swear I feel my clit tremble as his fingers wrap around my thigh and his fingertips near my folds.

I want to moan *yes, yes,* but I can't stop fucking his

mouth with my tongue as he pulls away and moves his mouth down to my right breast. He sucks my hardened nipple into his mouth through the fabric and flicks it with his tongue. He pauses long enough to whisper, "You're not wearing a bra," and moves back to my nipple. I whimper a moan into the silent darkness and grind hard against him.

"I had already gone back to my room for the night when... mmmm... I got a... call."

He lowers me back to the ground and uses both hands to lift my shirt above my breasts and his mouth moves to my left breast, this time skin on skin and I'm in ecstasy. I move my hand down to the massive bulge in his pants and stroke up and down.

"Are we going to do this?" I ask.

"I want to. I want you badly. I have for a long time."

"But you have barely ever looked at me." My head is swimming. Did the man I've had a massive crush on, for over two years, just say he's wanted me badly... for a long time?

"You work for me. Worked for me. What was I supposed to do?"

"Well, I don't work for you anymore, and I want you inside me." With one final stroke up his length, I unzip his pants and slip my hand inside his boxers to grasp his magnificent cock. "Do you have a condom?"

He pulls back. "No. Do you?"

"Shit. No."

"But we might die. What if we plunge to our deaths? Wouldn't you rather die with me inside you?"

"And if we don't?" I can't resist continuing to stroke his cock, and now it feels like I'm teasing him, but I don't stop. "I have a strict 'No Cover No Lover' policy."

"But we might die." I can tell he is playfully pleading with me, and I want him even more.

Another stroke down and his cock rubs up my forearm as I reach his swollen testicles and rub my fingers around them to their base. "Don't worry, there's still plenty of fun to be had."

"Damn right there is." He reaches down and grabs both of my arms by the wrists, raises them above my head and spins me in place to face away from him. He presses my hands high against the elevator wall and commands, "Don't move."

In an instant, he is working the zipper at the back of my skirt and pulling the sides to my feet, holding them until I step out. The power could come back on at any moment with me pinned, bare assed, against the elevator wall and I couldn't care less. I feel his hands glide up my legs and reach for my red lace panties. My mistake, I wasn't bare ass before… but I am now. And I was right. I don't give a shit.

His hands glide back up my legs again and up both sides of my ass with his thumbs near the center as he rises to stand behind me. "Your ass is as magnificent as I always hoped it would be."

All I can say is, "I'm glad you like..." before he slides his cock between the cheeks of my ass and presses into me. I finish my sentence with a groan as he reaches his right hand around my belly and slides his hand down to my wetness. His fingers slide up and down my folds, and I want to beg him to enter me. One finger, two, three, I don't care.

"Please," I say as he slides a finger inside me slow and forceful. I press my ass into his cock, but he pulls his finger out. "Please," I say again.

Smack. He swats my ass with the hand he just robbed me of, and I can't contain myself but I love it.

"Wow." I turn my head slightly. "I wasn't expecting that."

"Do you mind?"

"No." I can't believe what I'm saying.

"Good. Because I am going to make you come, and it won't take long, but I'm in charge. We go at my pace. Don't rush me. I promise you won't regret it." He presses his cock harder at me, up and down in the crevasse of my ass.

His left hand moves to my left breast, and he brushes his fingers across the top of my nipple. I am too distracted with the pleasure of the jarring to my hardened tip to notice his right hand is back at my wet opening again. The stretch of two fingers entering me snaps me out of it, and I struggle to catch my breath. And his thumb is at my clitoris to begin its work.

"Oh, yes," I cry out and arch my neck back into his mouth, and he kisses the back of my neck.

And he was right. It doesn't take long. This is a man who knows how to please a woman. His left hand works my nipple, his mouth nibbles on the back of my neck and he thrusts his fingers in and out, and in and out, while flicking my clit with his thumb. As I reach my climax, he is grinding hard into my ass, heightening his pleasure and mine as my insides clamp down again and again on his fingers. I feel how badly he wants to be inside me, and I want it too.

He stands behind me for several minutes, caressing my belly and nibbling at my neck as I catch my breath. Now it's my turn, or rather… his turn. I step to the side, spin around him, shove him against the elevator wall and force his arms up.

"Holy shit." He tries to turn to face me but I press his hands into the wall. "You're fast."

"Don't move." I am out of my mind and don't know what has come over me but I don't care. I can't have him inside me, but I can have some fun with him. I grab the sides of his pants and pull them down to his ankles, boxers and all. I mimic his run up my legs as I move my hands up his calves and thighs to his ass. "Your ass is as magnificent *as I* always hoped it would be."

As I stand, I reach around and grab his throbbing cock in my hand and shove my hips into his ass. "Oh wow…" he says as he glances back.

"Smack." I whack his tight right ass cheek and almost laugh at myself with how hard I hit him.

"Hey now…" He feigns a turn.

"Quiet," I say as I reach around and stroke his cock again. "Now I'm in charge, and you won't come until I say so."

"You are so going to pay for this."

"Promises, promises," I whisper in his ear.

I move my left hand between his legs, running my arm along the center of his ass as I reach his balls and caress them while continuing to stroke with my right hand.

"Oh my …" He moves to place his forehead against the wall of the elevator and his cock grows in my grip. I move my right hand to work the head of his cock while my left hand moves back and forth between his balls and the length of his shaft. As his forehead impacts the wall of the elevator, the lights come back on and the elevator lurches down.

"Oh shit." He turns and faces me. "Ah man, this isn't fair."

"Oh my god." I turn and bend over to grab my panties and my skirt.

"That's really not fair." I glance back over my shoulder to see him staring at my naked ass exposed right in front of his bulging cock.

I stand upright; begin pulling my clothes on and watch the numbers decline, praying we don't stop. "You better pull up your pants."

Eight, seven, six.

"Tuck your shirt in." I reach over and try to straighten his hair.

Five, Four, three.

"Your lipstick is all over your face." His thumb traces the outside of my lips in a hurried attempt to remove the smear, and a smile spreads across his face as he situates the pencil over my ear.

Two, L.

"Here, you need this." I hand him my leather planner and glance down at the massive bulge in his pants.

"Ding."

The elevator door opens just as he moves the planner down to cover his crotch. A crowd of our co-workers, heading to their rooms from the party wait to enter the elevator. "Michael." Alan Stephenson, the head of Network Development, remains outside the elevator as the others enter. "I've been looking for you. I tried you on your cell but you didn't answer. We have an emergency."

"We were…" Michael glances over at me. "We were stuck in the elevator."

Having been thrust back to reality, I am a little embarrassed and take my opportunity to escape. "Thanks, Michael." I point to my planner. "I'll need that back when you have everything… covered." I smile and turn to walk away.

"Lindsey," Michaels calls out.

I don't look back but wave over my shoulder.

"Lindsey…."

"Bye, Michael." If only he could see the smile on my face. Damn that was hot. He might need my planner for a week.

CHAPTER 4

Lindsey

I'VE TAKEN the elevator to my apartment countless times, and I know this time shouldn't be any different, but it is. I can't stop thinking of the most spectacular elevator trip in the history of humankind. I'm sure it's not weird at all to have the thought of a falling, powerless elevator send a warm wave down the core of my body that culminates with the memory of his hand… those fingers… and I feel his absence. I yearn for his touch, to feel his animal lust hover over me once more, his body screaming its desire to enter me, to have me. As the elevator doors open and I head toward my apartment, I feel the perma-smile on my face. I don't think it has left my face since I left Michael to his emergency.

Then I scurried out of Las Vegas first thing in the morning like a one-night-stand sneaking out the bedroom door.

No shame, just uncertainty.

Big deal. I told him a little white lie. I haven't quit my job yet but I want to. I'm sure I have to. Not because of him, not because of what happened, but for me, no matter how bad I want him and love being near him. Besides, he made it very clear he would never give me the time of day as long as I work for him. What did I have to lose?

And besides… oh shit! I just remembered I forgot to finish my email to Luke McKenna. The unfinished draft is still waiting to be sent when I open my email so I quickly finish my reply.

Luke,

Thank you so much for thinking of me. I…

I'm sorry for the delay, I got interrupted and had to handle an emergency. I would love to work with you. Let me know, as soon as you can, where you want to hold the event. We don't have a lot of time, if you have a particular venue in mind I will need to put down a deposit to hold the space.

. . .

CRAP. I don't even have a business name. So I pull one out of thin air and close the email with:

Superior Events and Occasions, Inc.
Lindsey Laverly, CEO

SOUNDS like a winning name to me. I should probably make sure nobody else is using that name, but for now I'm still having trouble thinking of anything but my rendezvous with Michael. So I projected my desire to leave and start my own business forward in time, and I don't even have as much as one signed contract yet. I couldn't help myself. When I realized he wanted me as much as I wanted him, I kind of lost control of my senses. Who could blame a girl? I have animal lust of my own after all and it just took over for a while. He's hot, smart, nice, sexy, rich and… oh yeah… hot.

I still haven't regained control of my senses. I am transfixed on that moment and I swear I can still feel his cock in my hand; his burning rage for my bod radiating from every pore, but as I glance down at that hand, I see that I only hold my phone and the keys to my apartment. I have no idea how long I've been standing here, but I glance to my right to notice my neighbor Penny outside her door watching me, and I grin sheepishly her way.

"Hey, Lindsey."

"Hi, Penny." I shake my head as I come back to my senses.

"Everything okay?"

"Oh yeah." I smile, put the key in the door, turn the handle and enter my apartment.

I hear Penny holler from down the hall. "Good weekend?"

"Oh boy." I holler back as I close my door. I know she wants details and maybe I'll tell her, maybe not. This one was special. Besides, if I tell anyone before I tell Bethany, she will kill me.

I leave my suitcase at the door, head to the kitchen and open the refrigerator door. Milk, apples, oranges, cheese; I'm not really hungry so I head to the couch and grab the TV remote. Before the screen finishes lighting, I hit the power button again to turn it off and reach for the magazine on my coffee table. As I flip through pages I don't even see and am not interested in, I feel my heart pounding in my chest. It hasn't stopped since the elevator ride and not the one I just took; the most amazing elevator ride ever… in the history of mankind. I haven't been able to sleep ever since, that's why I hopped on an earlier flight out of Vegas than I was scheduled for.

I stand for no apparent reason and look around my apartment.

Enough of this nonsense; what's better for those moments when your heart is throbbing in your chest than a cup of coffee? I need to escape this lonely apartment. Get Perky coffee shop here I come. I grab my keys again, and I am out the door. This time I take the stairs.

When I open the door to Get Perky, the familiar bell rings and the aroma of ground coffee beans welcomes me like a second home. I feel better in an instant and my mind is relieved of every other thought but my menu options for the day. Cinnamon spiced latte, vanilla skinny latte or a caramel macchiato… decisions, decisions. My favorite, cute, young barista is behind the counter and smiles as he watches me approach.

"Hey, Chris." I love flirting with him because it gets me free pastries.

"Hey, troublemaker."

"Me?"

"Yeah you. You told me your friend thought I was hot." He shakes his head at me.

I can't help but laugh a little as I recall my mischievous deed. "Well, I'm sure she thinks so, all the girls do."

"Whatever… she's engaged. Thanks a lot; it made me look like an egomaniac."

"Oh she's not really engaged, she doesn't even like the guy."

"Well, she blew me off with the wave of her ring, and I looked like a bonehead, so you are in trouble."

"Oh, you still love me, Chris." I raise my left eyebrow to tease him. "Can I get a cinnamon spice latte?"

I raise my phone to the scanner and pay for my latte before moving down to the end of the counter to wait, hoping he will include a complimentary scone like usual, though I may have pushed too far last time. I don't think he's too serious.

An adorable gray-haired little old lady I'm sure I recognize walks toward me after placing her order. She is wearing a perfectly matched red outfit with red leather gloves, red heels and matching bright red lipstick.

"Hello," I say as she nears the end of the counter.

"Oh hello, dear. How are you today?" Her smile brightens the whole store and my day, and I remember where I've seen her before.

"I'm good. Aren't you a friend of Bethany's?" I ask.

"Oh yes, she's a wonderful girl. You're her friend Lindsey, right?"

"Yes, nice to meet you." I'm shocked to think they talked of me and she remembered my name. I reach out to shake her hand and she removes her gloves before grabbing my hand. The warmth in her touch is instant and calming. "Has Bethany spoken of me?"

"I'm sure she must have. I know we are friends already." She smiles, glances around the store and points to an empty table for two. "Would you like to have coffee with me?"

"Umm sure. That would be great."

Chris is busy filling orders but calls over the

counter. "Go ahead and have a seat, Opal. I'll bring your drinks over to you."

"Oh thank you, honey." Opal waves to him and heads to a two-seat table. As we take our seats Opal meticulously folds her coat and gloves before smoothing her skirt and sitting. I'm beginning to think she knows everyone.

"You know Chris?"

"Oh sure, he's such a nice young man, and he takes such good care of me."

I'm certain Opal is the type of person to never say a bad thing about anyone, the type of grace that comes with old school manners, manners that seem to have been forgotten in our fast-paced, high-tech world. I find her refreshing, and my mood has improved just by sitting across from her.

"So how did you and Bethany meet?" I ask her.

"Oh let's talk about us, that will be much more fun. Tell me, how was your weekend?"

It's like I can't help but spill the beans on my weekend, and I don't stop there. I blab about the entire status of my life, and before I realize it, a half hour has passed, my latte is nearly empty and Opal has barely said a word. Oh she asks questions... then listens, then asks more questions... and listens more. I'm in love with her already. I used to have conversations like this when my grandma was alive, and I'd almost forgotten how much I miss our talks. Somehow my grandmother always guided me to the right decision by asking questions and listening without offering her own opinion or answers. I always left her knowing just what I needed to do.

"What do you want to do? What will be best for you?" Opal asks.

"I feel like I have to quit my job and take a risk. I want my own company, so I can prove myself and really make something of my life."

"And what of this young man, Michael? He sounds wonderful."

"I think he is but we can never date if I work for him; he won't allow it. And I feel if I leave, I will never see him again, and he will just forget about me."

"So what do you think is the right thing to do?"

"My heart tells me that I need to do what is right for me and become the success I always felt I would be. And if things with Michael are meant to be, something, I don't know, magical, will have to happen."

"Oh, honey, I agree. You seem like a very smart and capable person. I'm sure you will be a success and everything else will fall into place."

"I hope so because I kind of told him a little white lie. I told him I quit, even though I haven't yet." I glance down at the last bit of coffee in my cup and feel a little shame as I tell this sweet little old lady about my lie.

"It wasn't a lie. You were just setting things in motion."

"That's a very generous interpretation of events." I

glance back up at her with a guilty smile. "But I think I'll go with that, only what if I become a success and that turns him off. I've read that some men lose their attraction to a woman who becomes successful in business."

"Have faith, dear, in yourself and in him. In my experience, a successful woman does not intimidate any man worth his salt or one worth having."

I take my final sip of coffee and say to myself, into my cup, "And the rest have tiny little hands."

"What was that?"

Thank goodness she didn't hear me. "Oh nothing."

"It's been so nice talking to you, but I really must run." Opal stands and sets her gloves on the table while she puts on her coat.

I reach for the red gloves and hand them to her after she finishes positioning her coat. "Here you go. Thank you so much for the talk, it's so nice to meet you."

Opal reaches out and takes my hands into hers. "Believe in yourself, honey. You have what it takes to reach your dreams, have faith in yourself and the world will move in mysterious ways to help you achieve your goals. All of them." The warmth of her touch runs through my hands, up my arms, spreads to my chest and I find myself speechless, captured by her gaze.

"Hey, Opal." I turn to see my best friend Bethany calling to Opal and walking our way.

"Oh hello, dearie." Opal smiles and turns as she greets Bethany.

"New gloves?" Bethany asks Opal.

"Oh no, I have a matching pair for every outfit." Opal reaches out and grabs Bethany's hand. "Everything turned out just wonderful, didn't it?"

"Better than wonderful." An attractive man walks up beside Bethany, but he does not look anything like her former fiancé. He's much hotter and sexier with tattoos that run out the collar of his shirt and up the base of his neck. This must be the guy, her hot stud from work and, oh yeah, from the Christmas party. "I want you to meet someone." Bethany directs Opal to the hot guy now standing next to her.

Opal seems as though she already knows him and reaches out with her free hand to grab his hand. "Well hello, Zach."

"Hello." He looks down at her hand and smiles at her touch.

Bethany's look is confusion and she asks him, "Have you two met?" But Opal interrupts.

"You two make such a lovely couple." Opal releases their hands and begins to put on her gloves. "I couldn't be happier for you. I know you'll be very happy together." Then she turns and smiles at me. "Honey, I enjoyed our conversation so much. Remember what I said. We'll meet again."

I turn to watch as she walks to the door. An elderly

gentleman opens the door and holds it for her while she passes through and disappears.

"Who was that?" Zach asks.

I rise from my table, look to the door and answer, "That's Opal, she's delightful."

Bethany turns to me and says, "That's what I said, delightful."

Zach is staring at the door like he is lost in a dream. "She was delightful, wasn't she?"

Cute barista Chris walks our way and hands Zach two drinks. "Here's your coffee, Zach."

"Thanks, Chris." Zach takes the cups from him and hands one to Bethany.

As Zach hands Bethany her drink, I can't help but notice a huge rock on her left ring finger. Holy shit. Is she engaged again? Already? "What the hell is this?" Without even thinking, I grab her hand and yank it to my face. "What is this rock quarry on your finger? You bitch, you didn't. Why didn't you tell me?"

"It just happened this morning. We haven't had a chance to tell anyone yet."

I am so happy for her I can't contain myself, so I scream, grab Zach in a giant hug and shake him so hard he spills his coffee. "Welcome to the family, big guy." I look over and see my best friend, blissful in happiness, and pull her into my embrace. "We're going to be so happy." I shake Bethany so hard she spills her coffee too.

Chris looks at the floor and sighs, "I guess I'm going

to have to clean that up." He shakes his head at me and walks away. "I knew you two were going to be so much trouble."

We smile at each other and yell in unison. "Sorry, Chris."

I couldn't be happier for Bethany. She is super sweet, kind and the best of best friends; she deserves to be happy. Goodness knows her previous fiancé didn't fulfill her needs. But by the look on Zach's face and the glow emanating from her, these two both meet each other's needs just fine.

Bethany and Zach pull away from my hug assault, hook arms and Bethany says, "You have to come out with us; I can't have a best friend who doesn't even know my future husband. We have to go out to dinner."

"Let's do it." I wag my finger at Zach. "I'll have to thoroughly interrogate you before you have final approval."

"Can you do tomorrow night?" Bethany asks.

"I leave for Hawaii tomorrow remember." I take a week at the end of each year to unwind on the beach. This year's beach of choice is in Hawaii and I can't wait. I have a lot of thinking to do.

"I forgot, you delayed your trip this year because of the Las Vegas thing."

"Yep, and I still have to go home and pack, so I better get going."

"Call me when you get back." Bethany snuggles into Zach's side and sips her coffee.

"I will. Nice to meet you, Zach." I head out the door and my mind spins into overdrive. I'm thrilled for Bethany. She deserves a great guy and all the happiness she always wanted. And now, more than ever, I am certain it's time for me to get moving toward all the happiness I've always wanted.

CHAPTER 5

Michael

I ALWAYS PARK my car in the last row of the rear parking lot for our office and always feel a little silly doing so. There are plenty of spaces closer to the building, hell, I have a reserved spot in the front row, but as usual, I find myself looking for every opportunity to interject a little exercise into my day. When I arrived at the airport last night, I carried my luggage instead of rolling it on its perfectly capable wheels. I don't know why I bother, but I do; I can't help that I don't know how to be lazy.

I unzip my jacket as I walk toward the building to feel the cold morning air on my chest. The sensation of the crisp winter air envelops me in its grasp and slaps me awake. I've never minded getting up and going to work, even on Monday mornings. It's not as though I'm one of those annoying eternally happy people who bubble disgusting enthusiasm twenty-four-seven; I just love a challenge. I have to be challenged or I get incredibly bored. Everyone assumes that owning your own company; especially a tech startup is peaches and cream, rainbows and unicorns with a pot of gold and a magical leprechaun farting fairy dust your way. Nothing could be further from the truth. A tech start up is incredibly hard, incredibly risky and very stressful; often times I'm miserable, but I can't live without it. Besides, I'm pretty sure those bubbly disgusting people go home and drink themselves stupid every night.

Normally, when I head into the office after a long absence, an entire array of a to-do list runs through my mind, but not today. Today I can only think of Lindsey. I haven't been able to get her out of my mind since that fucking elevator ride. Not an elevator ride from hell that one might expect after losing power and nearly plunging to one's death. This brush with death was pure heaven; ecstasy in a six by eight metal box and my dick has been hard ever since, if not physically, for sure metaphorically. I still feel her touch and inhale her scent with every breath.

After passing through the employee entrance, I turn left rather than my usual route straight up the middle to my office. I have to go by her desk. I have to see her.

A right turn down the last aisle and I look ahead, hoping to see her busy at her desk. She is nowhere in sight. Shit. How many times will I have to make an excuse to come this way today before I catch her at her desk? Upon reaching her office, I pause and look around; her desk hasn't been touched. Is she not here yet?

"Good morning, Mr. Sinclair." Oh good, it's her assistant. Perfect timing.

"Hey, Chad. Have you seen Lindsey? I need to talk to her."

"No, she's not here. Is there something you need? I'm sure I can do it for you." Geez this guy can lay it on thick. I never understood why Lindsey hired him, he's such a kiss ass and he doesn't even try to hide it. It's not his offer of help that is annoying, it's the way he says it that makes me want to wrap my hands around his skinny neck.

"Where is she?"

"Oh she won't be in; she's on vacation this week."

"Vacation? Did she leave directly from Las Vegas? I looked for her yesterday morning at the hotel but I couldn't find her." The truth is I stalked the lobby all morning but never caught sight of her. I nearly missed my flight I waited so long.

"Oh she went standby on an early flight and left me to take care of business at the hotel, but don't worry I took care of everything." Chad crosses his arms and furrows his brow in an apparent attempt to display competency. "Though it wasn't easy. There was a lot to do."

"Do you know where she went?"

"I have no idea, sir. She doesn't communicate very well, but I find a way to take care of things for her anyway. Whatever you need, I'm sure I can take care of it for you."

"I don't think so, Chad." If only he knew. "Okay, thanks."

Chad continues to talk as I walk away, but I ignore him and my mind returns to Lindsey. Did she give notice and then quit to use up the last of her vacation? Will she ever be back? What if I never see her again? I have to see her again.

As I reach the front of the building, I pass by the main conference room and head for my office. My assistant Janice is standing, with her tablet in hand, waiting for me.

"Where did you come from?" She asks as she follows me into my office.

"What do you mean? I come that way sometimes, to say good morning to some of the employees first."

"You never come that way; you never make the rounds before your morning briefing."

"Well, I'm turning over a new leaf."

"Uh huh." Janice has worked with me too long. She knows when I'm bullshitting. "Let's just say I believe you and get on with it."

"Sounds good. Shall we get started?" My mornings

always begin with a rundown of current issues and a preview of scheduled events for the day. I couldn't survive without Janice; she's my work wife, but I call her my work mom, and she hates when I say so because she is only a few years older than I am. She is invaluable; she keeps me focused and headed in the right direction.

"Yes, let's do." And she begins. "Alan emailed you this morning to say your solution to the network issue seems to have worked, no further problems. And…"

Janice continues to talk, but I don't hear a word she says. All I can think of is Lindsey and that elevator. I can only think of touching the skin of her supple belly, her nipple under my fingertips, her pussy clinching on my fingers… her hand on my cock…

"And the quick brown fox jumps over the lazy dog and I turned a trick on a trip to tinsel town in a teeny tiny tank top." Janice isn't reading from her tablet, and she stops to stare at me with an exasperated look on her face.

"What?"

"You're not paying attention. You obviously didn't hear a word I said."

"Yes I am."

"What did I just say?"

"I'm afraid to say, something about a tank top."

"Exactly what I thought."

"Can we pick this up later?" I get up from my chair.

"What's going on, Michael?"

"What?" I say as I begin to head for the door. "Nothing."

"I know this look." She rises and follows me out the door. "What happened this weekend?"

"Nothing. I'll be back in awhile."

"You have meetings this morning."

"Cancel them," I call out as I walk away, back towards Lindsey's office.

As I pass the conference room again and turn the corner, Chad jumps up from his chair and is already talking at me again but I interrupt. "Chad I need to know where Lindsey is."

"I'm sorry, sir, but I don't know where she went."

"Who might know?"

"I have no idea."

"Think, Chad. Think. Your job may depend on it."

I'm only messing with him, but I swear he nearly shits himself. "She meets her best friend at the same coffee shop almost every day around eleven o'clock."

"Which one?"

"That little shop a couple blocks down, its called Get Perky. Let me get the address for you." Chad leans over his computer. "Yep, this is the one and I was right, it is just down the street. The address is 1418 John Street."

Before he finishes, I am on my way out the door. I know the exact coffee shop because I drive by it every day. Chad calls out from behind me as I go, "Sir, if you want me to go get coffee and wait for her friend I will, I can bring you back a latte."

I cover the two blocks to the small coffee shop in no time flat, swing open the door and lunge through like a mad man. I must look like one too because everyone in the store turns and watches me as I scan all the tables. I realize I have no idea what I'm looking for, and that I look like a crazy man, so I try to settle down and blend in by getting in the ordering line. The young guy at the register does not seem in a hurry and for some reason feels the need to have a conversation with every customer. I wish he would speed the hell up. I'm in a hurry here. What if I missed her already?

"Can I help you?" Finally it's my turn.

"Yes, do you know Lindsey?"

"I'm sorry, what?" The kid's nametag looks like it was written by a kindergartner but reads "Chris".

"Chris, do you know Lindsey? She comes in here all the time and meets her best friend."

"Yeah, I know Lindsey."

I make a hurried look around the store. "Is her best friend here? I'm Lindsey's boss, and I was hoping she might be able to tell me where Lindsey went on vacation. It's really important. Mission critical, if you know what I mean." I can't believe I said such a stupid thing, I don't even 'know what I mean'.

"You're way too early. They don't usually come in until around eleven."

And it dawns on me. In my haste, I stormed out of

the office and didn't pay attention to the time. "Shit." I put my hands on the counter and shake my head.

"Did you want to order something? You're welcome to wait."

I don't want to seem like the jerk who held up the line for nothing, so I order, "Large black coffee".

"That will be $3.59."

I pull a twenty-dollar bill out of my wallet and hand it to him. "Keep the change."

"Thanks." Chris puts the change in the tip jar. "You know, Opal talks to Lindsey and her friend all the time. She might be able to help you."

"Opal?" I ask.

Chris nods and points toward the main entrance. "The woman in purple sitting by herself."

"Thanks, Chris, you're the man."

"That's what they tell me."

I turn and spot an elderly woman seated at a table and she is alone. She is dressed in bright purple from head to toe and looks me in the eyes the entire time I walk toward her. I smile to gauge her mood but she doesn't smile back, she looks me over, from head to toe, as I approach. She is facing my direction with her legs crossed under her skirt and her hands clasped over her knees holding a pair of matching purple gloves. I can feel a lump forming in my throat, and I'm not sure because I'm afraid to check, but sweat may be beading on my brow. This could be a dead end. "Hi." My voice squeaks as I speak, so I attempt to clear my throat and try again. "I was talking to Chris over there and he said you might be able to help me."

"Of course I can, have a seat." She motions to the chair across from her and I sit. "You're even more handsome than I thought you'd be." Her voice is kind and reassuring with a touch of a mid-western accent.

I am totally confused. "I'm sorry… do I…"

She reaches across to shake my hand and she smiles; a smile that starts at her brightly painted red lips, rises up to her high cheekbones and spreads as a twinkle in her deeply green eyes. "I'm Opal." The warmth of her touch rises into my chest and the anxiety I felt instantly dissipates.

"I was wondering if you might know how I can find—"

"Listen, Michael." How does she know me? My mind spins back, trying to remember. Did I freaking black out on my way over to the table and she lifted my wallet before reviving me? Is it written across my forehead? Is she a wizard? "You want to know about Lindsey."

"Uhhh. Yes?"

"Let's talk about your intentions."

"Ma'am?"

"That's right, Michael." She sits back and crosses her arms. "Let's hear it. What are your intentions with Lindsey?"

I have to confess. "I hadn't really thought very far ahead."

She nods her head as though she knew all along. "Well, now is as good a time as any."

So I spill the beans. "I haven't been able to take my eyes off her since she started working for me. I make excuses to walk by her desk every chance I get, just to get a glimpse of her. And it's been agonizing because I have a very strict policy for myself. No dating employees. So I've been stuck in the misery of being near her every day, but unable to do anything about it. I couldn't even say anything. Then we got stuck in an elevator together and she told me she was quitting. We finally got to touch and—"

"Details aren't necessary, Michael."

I feel my face flush. "I haven't been able to think of anything else since. I can't even focus on work, on my business."

Opal leans over the table and looks at me intently. "She is a very intelligent woman. How do you feel about that? Some men are threatened by a smart woman."

"That's the thing that I find most attractive about her," I assure her. "And she's tough."

"She is also very ambitious. She has plans of her own you know."

"That's an absolute must," I respond.

"And if she becomes a great success? Will you support—"

"In any way I can," I interrupt.

Opal leans back and stares at me for what feels like an eternity. "You'll find her in Hawaii, Kauai Island."

I jump to my feet without thinking. "Thank you so much."

Opal joins me in standing and grabs my hand again. "It was a pleasure to meet you, Michael. Don't forget, I'll be keeping an eye on you."

"The pleasure was mine, ma'am."

A man appears from behind me and grabs Opal's overcoat. His dress is plain with a look out of the 1940s, working class church clothes in sepia tones. He's clean-shaven with short hair that looks like he just came from a visit to the barbershop. Straight up no-nonsense. Opal turns as he places her coat over her shoulders. "Have a nice trip, Michael."

I have no idea where this guy just came from, and I am at a loss for words as I watch him hold the door for her and they disappear outside.

I guess I'm going to Hawaii.

CHAPTER 6

Lindsey

IT DOESN'T GET any better than this; seventy-eight degrees with a light breeze coming off the ocean, the warmth of the sun on my skin and the thought of everybody back home freezing their 'you know what' off. And Sex on the Beach, unfortunately only the drink in my hand, not actual sex on the beach... with my boss. Even so, there is nothing like Hawaii in the wintertime.

As I lie and watch another day of surf lessons play out in front of me, the hotel's resident surf instructor, Colton, smiles in my direction. He's blond and very cute with a great body, tanned from head to toe and zero body fat. But he's young and only just smart enough to be a… well, a surf instructor for a hotel. Yes, he's hot, but it's hard to take him too serious; he's no Michael.

In my mind, I'm still in that elevator. Hell, I may never leave that elevator. Have they invented that virtual reality yet? I may have to talk to Michael about that when I get back; he should make *that* his next startup.

I'm daydreaming again and staring at nothing in particular but Colton thinks I'm watching him. "Hey, Lindsey." The two kids he is giving dry land instruction to turn my direction after he waves at me.

Uggh. I try to hide my irritation as I wave back, "Hey, Colton." I purposefully turn away and shake my head at my carelessness; I don't mean to encourage him, he certainly doesn't require it. I swear I must be at that point in my cycle. Not 'that time of the month' point but ovulating or something because Colton has been pursuing me like a tour bus full of seniors hunts a luau and a lei.

"Are you going to keep pretending like you're not watching me, or are we going out tonight?" Colton left his apprentice surfers to practice their moves and is standing over me before I can object.

"Shouldn't you be teaching them your rad moves?"

"I'd rather be showing you my rad moves."

"Seriously, Colton. What is it that you think you are going to do with me?" I look up at him and block the sun with my hand.

"How about I give you a lesson, on the house. Then we can decide what I am going to do with you. Come on, Lindsey, you'll have fun. I promise I'm a nice guy."

"I think you are anything but a nice guy." I put my hand down and look away.

"A lot of girls like that."

"I'm sure they do."

"Just one lesson, no strings attached. Depending on how good you are, we'll decide where I take you from there."

At that ridiculous comment I have to look up again and block the sun… again. "Seriously, you're going with that line."

"Yep. What do you say?"

I shake my head and turn to look for the waiter. I raise my empty drink glass and motion for another. I am not having sex on the beach with this guy, but who am I to turn down a free surfing lesson. "Fine, tomorrow. What time?"

"How 'bout after lunch. I'm free for the rest of the day after my morning lesson."

"Fine, now go away. You're blocking my sun."

"Awesome," he says as he turns and heads back to the brother and sister waiting for further 'rad' instruction. "You won't regret it. You'll like it and you're going to love me."

I can't help but think to myself, *I hardly think so,* but I smile and nod as he walks away. Who knows? Maybe I'll like surfing, him…not so much.

CHAPTER 7

Michael

I SUPPOSE if you are conducting a full-scale manhunt there are worse places to be, though I'm fucking exhausted. The flight to Kauai is a long ass flight. I haven't slept in forever, and I've spent two days wandering from hotel to hotel looking for a tourist in a haystack full of tourists. Still, it is Hawaii. The beauty of this island is second to none, and thank god, it's not very big. If I keep bribing hotel receptionists, I am bound to stumble across the right hotel eventually.

And who turns off their cell phone these days? I mean… I know she is on vacation and everything, but, sweet lord of tech-dependency, turn on your damn phone, Lindsey. You're missing something very important... Me.

Another right turn in my crappy rental car and here we go again. *Shit, shit, shit.* What is this hotel attempt number ten, twenty, ten thousand? Who cares? I lost track a long time ago, and soon I am going to have to find an ATM for more bribing cash. And what's with this barely functioning air conditioning in this tiny damn car. I can almost hear Janice laughing her ass off back at the office as I sweat through my shirt. She loves to mess with me. It's like a contest with her each time she reserves a car for me; can she get me in a worse vehicle than last time. Says it keeps me humble. Next time she'll have me in the last functioning Yugo left in the world.

I glance at the monument sign as I roll into the packed parking lot and pull in the first open spot I find. Ah the St. Regis, you look like a lucky hotel, you're bound to temporarily house a young, hot elevator temptress. I barely notice the greeter as I pass through the large glass doors to enter the lobby and give a quick, "No thanks," dodge as he attempts to yoke me with a lei. *I've got a car full already,* I think to myself, *and I'm not yoking.*

Great, now I'm resorting to telling myself bad jokes.

I pause to consider whether I may be truly losing it or just need some serious sleep and relief washes over me when I spot an available clerk awaiting my approach, fake smile and all. At least I don't have to wait in line… again.

"Good afternoon, sir. How can I help you?" I move toward the smiling, pale, freckle-faced red-headed young man swimming in a too-big sport coat emblazoned with the hotel logo and plaster my own fake smile on my face. "Are we checking in today?"

"Well that depends if you can help me." I feel like I'm in a bad romance movie scene every time I try this, but here I go again.

"I'll do my best, sir."

"I'm looking for someone, a Lindsey Laverly. I was wondering if you could tell me if she is staying here?"

"I'm sorry, sir, I'm not permitted to divulge any information about our guests."

In anticipation of his response, I have my wallet open, pull a hundred-dollar bill out and slide it across the counter. "I was hoping you might make an exception."

Red Regis glances side to side and smirks at me while he slides the money back my way and I pick it up. "I'm sorry, Mr. Laverly, I can't tell you if your wife is staying here."

Did he just call me Mr. Laverly? I instantly want to smack the freckled smirk right off his face. "Not Mr. Laverly; she's not my wife, she's an employee."

"I still can't tell you if she is a guest here." Not sure what my next move should be, it's my last bit of cash, I turn to walk away as I put the bill back in my wallet.

"But I may be able to tell you if she is not staying here."

"That would be great."

"Mmmm hmmm." Red clears his throat after glancing side to side again and eyeballs the former resting place of the hundred-dollar bill.

"You want me to… just to tell me she is not staying here?"

Red raises an eyebrow and glances down again. "If… she's not staying here."

I slide the money across the counter, and he palms it faster than I can say, "Fine, can you tell me if Lindsey…"

Before I say Laverly, his search is complete and my cash is in his pocket. "There is no Mrs. Laverly currently registered as a guest at this hotel."

"And you couldn't have just told me that… for free?"

"Is there anything else I can help you with?"

Now I'm exhausted and exasperated, I raise my finger at him and prepare to verbally violate the little grifter but I just exhale and walk away.

"You have a wonderful day, sir." He must feel a little guilty because he continues. "If Mrs. Laverly is here for a relaxing… tryst, you might check the hotels in Nawiliwili Bay. It's much quieter this time of year. Most people staying in the north right now are here for the big wave competition."

"Thanks," I call over my shoulder as I head toward my rental car and pull out my cell phone to begin my search for hotels in Nawiliwili Bay. Packed with hotels and a little less than an hour away means I may have just enough time to call in logistical support. Right now I can't think of a better reason to have a team of hackers in my employ... which one can I trust not to blab to the whole company?

CHAPTER 8

*L*indsey

WHY DID I agree to this? I came to Hawaii prepared to relax in the sun, improve my tan and catch up on some reading, not take surf lessons from a barely post-pubescent, dim-witted horn dog. And the only swim suits I brought consist of colored variations of the same teeny tiny bikini. I have to admit, as I stand in front of the mirror in my room, I look damn good in the red version I am wearing, too good. Yes, it's small, but I never meant for it to hold everything together while jumping up and down on a surfboard. Sometimes having boobs can be a real pain. I turn to the side to gauge how badly the girls are bulging out the sides and notice the strings on the sides of the bottoms look like they will come untied at any moment. I continue to turn and look at my behind in the mirror and smack myself in the forehead. What an idiot I am, I'm nearly flossing just standing here.

But I do look good.

What can I say? My only thought was minimizing tan lines, not holding back the sea.

No way, I can't do it. As I walk to my suitcase in the corner of my room, I can only think of excuses for why I shouldn't go. My room is so nice and quiet and comfortable. The bed, covered in white linens, is huge and inviting. The sliding glass doors are open and lead to a balcony overlooking the beach; the smell of the ocean blowing past the curtains fills the room as the rumble of the incoming waves beats like a metronome. I could just lie down and take a nap and forget about Colton, hope he forgets that I'm here.

Yeah, like that will happen.

Fine. I'll take his stupid lesson just so I can get him to leave me alone. But not dressed like this. I dive into my suitcase and cover myself with a t-shirt and gym shorts, pull my hair into a ponytail and head back to the closet door for a visual update.

Ahhh. Much better.

I smile at the boring, plain Jane tourist lady in the mirror then slip into my flip-flops, and I am out the door.

My room is only a few feet from the stairs that lead to the main floor. As I round the corner and head into the lobby, you know who is chatting up the young female serving drinks at the bar. She is smiling like a flirty schoolgirl while typing into a cell phone. Colton smiles in my direction, grabs the phone from the bartender and rushes to catch me as I walk toward the front door.

"Hey, Lindsey. You ready?" Colton calls out as he lumbers in a lazy, lanky, surfer boy jog in my direction.

"You finished over there?" I ask. "I didn't interrupt, did I?"

"Oh that's Lucy; she's new here. Just introducing myself."

"You get her number?" I grin and raise a single eyebrow at him to let him know I am wise to his game.

"What? No. She just asked if she could borrow my phone to look something up."

"Sure, Colton." I shrug, because I really couldn't care less. Much less than he can possibly imagine. I just wish he would lay off the constant full-court press on me. "Where do we start this lesson?"

Colton stops and looks me up and down. "That what you're wearing?"

I come to a screeching halt and he has to dodge to avoid running into me. "Is this a problem?"

"No. No, I just—"

"Just what, Colton?"

"Well, it is hot outside, and I will make you hot and sweaty." He can barely contain a stupid shit-eating grin."

I head out the door and he follows. "Trust me, Colton. I can handle anything you throw at me. Try not to get too excited. This is just a surfing lesson. That's it."

"But it is a surf lesson. You do know you have to get in the water and that means you will get wet. You'll need a swim suit." He smiles and nods like he has just proven a court winning case.

"Let's cross that bridge when we come to it." I pause, motion for him to lead the way, then follow.

I hate to admit it but within thirty minutes of oral instruction, jumping up and down on a beached surfboard and endless amounts of surfer boy wisdom, I am having a good time. Colton seems to know what he is talking about and has enough experience and patience to come off as a professional as long as he forgets that his main goal is getting in my pants. When he's not trying so hard, he can be quite charming. He has a great smile and a naturally easy-going manner about him. And damn it, he is very good-looking with an amazing body. Before long, I forget myself and begin to let my defenses down.

"This is not easy to say but, Colton, you were right." I fan my t-shirt to move some air across my body. "It's hot and I'm sweating like a Southerner in a Saturday flea market."

"Well, I think you are almost ready to get in Mother Ocean. You did wear a suit under there, right?"

I can't put it off any longer, so I nod and begin to

pull my t-shirt over my head. "No comments." I stop and point at him while giving him a half-hearted evil eye. He feigns fear and makes a zipping motion across his lips. But, as the t-shirt comes off and I bend over to pull off my shorts, he can't help himself upon full view of my bikini. "Oh, man. Now that is a swimsuit. This is going to be perfect. We should do a couple more practice runs and then head out."

Of course he makes me do more than a couple practice attempts. I'm sure I look ridiculous as I struggle to keep my boobs from falling out while jumping to my feet. And with each attempt, his voice lowers an octave.

"Mmmm, looking good."

Before long, he is like a villain from a B-movie, one arm crossed while the other strokes a goatee he doesn't have, nodding and surveying his prey. "One more time." He says and now *he* is sweating. "You're almost ready for the water."

I figure I better stop him before he ends up with a full-on erection. "I think I've got it, Colton." I reach over and give him a sarcastic, reassuring shoulder tap. "You need to cool off, let's get in the water."

"Hello, Lindsey." A very familiar masculine voice calls from behind me, and as I turn to see the man behind the voice walking across the sand, I am speechless.

"Michael?"

CHAPTER 9

*M*ichael

THANK god I didn't have to search every hotel in Nawiliwili Bay to find out where Lindsey is staying. Within thirty minutes of enlisting the help of my best programmers, they had a lead for me. I don't know how they did it and, frankly, I don't want to know. Every programmer worth his paycheck is a hacker at heart and I employ some of the best. Alan texted me to let me know that Lindsey's phone hasn't been turned on in two days but the last time it was she was at the Garden Isle Hotel and Spa. As I pull into the parking lot, I realize I haven't really thought about what I will say, and I notice a strange sensation in my chest. I don't think I've ever had this feeling before.

I think I am panicking. Is that what this is? And what the hell am I doing here?

And. And. And, what the hell am I going to say? *Hey, Lindsey baby. So... I know we've worked together and... I've barely said two words to you... and even though I've been attracted to you forever, you probably never noticed my constant staring because I didn't, I couldn't. I couldn't risk it. And then we almost had sex in that elevator... the best almost sex I've ever had... hell, better than any actual sex I've ever had. And I haven't been able to stop thinking about you. And I think I'm in love with you. Uuu... gh.*

Her answer will no doubt be *Step away, you stalker psycho who followed me all the way to Hawaii. I'm calling the police.*

And so I sit in my horrible rental car, sweating and frozen at the same time, my back is beginning to stick to the fake leather seats when my right hand begins to tingle. I'm reminded of my talk with Opal, that adorable elderly woman from the coffee shop, and I know what I have to do. I am out the car door in a flash and on a mission. I have to find her. She has to be here and she has to be mine.

As I trek across the parking lot, hope and happiness swell in my chest. I know I am doing the right thing and that Lindsey has only been thinking of me too, waiting for me. She has to be. I know we are meant for each other and I can't wait to find her.

She'll probably want to know why it took me so long to get here.

I pull open the hotel door and a wash of cool welcoming air envelops and invites me to enter. This has to be the right place; I can almost sense her presence.

Even the sight of the long line of customers waiting to check in doesn't deflate my optimism. It will give me time to think of a reason why they should confirm that she is staying here and, for the love of god, tell me where she is. I take my place in the back of the line and my mind races with excitement; I glance out the back door of the lobby that leads to the beach and up jumps Lindsey, arms out like she's flying. What the hell is going on? She does know she's on the sand, doesn't she?

And then I notice him.

Who's the penis with a tan and why is he holding my girl's hand helping her balance... on the sand?

I'm frozen again.

Before I realize I've moved zombie style through the sliding doors, I am on the back patio of the hotel, staring in disbelief.

They are talking and laughing and he's... he's teaching her how to surf. How gross. I guess I was wrong about the 'only thinking of me thing'. Should I just turn around and leave her to him? Did I come all this way for nothing?

I think I'm going to be sick.

I grab a seat and watch in horror.

Before I know it, the crisis escalates. She undressed

BILLIONAIRE'S OBSESSION

in front of him and is now practically naked in one of the tiniest bikinis I have ever seen. His eyes are feasting on her amazing body, and now I'm getting pissed, but damn does she look good. I'm getting a better look at more of what I missed in that elevator. I feel my cock begin to lengthen, and I think I'm not the only one. Mr. Tanned God of Cockdom is hanging back, drinking in every move of her voluptuous body as she rises and falls at his command.

I can't take it any longer. I have to do something. Shit is not going down this way. But first... I need a drink; I need to look composed, casual and carefree.

Sure, idiot. You flew all the way to Hawaii because you are carefree.

"Waiter," I yell. "Rum and coke on the rocks, hold the coke."

I sit and I stew and I watch. Just as the waiter returns with my drink, the scrotum with a totem closes the gap and pauses her training.

Shit, looks like they are getting ready to go into the water.

It's now or never. Time to make my move and claim my territory, back this motherfucker off. I'm up and moving across the sand before I've even contemplated what to say. *Oh, hey, Lindsey, you here too? Crazy, baby. Oh, yeah I come here all the time. What a coincidence. Blah blah blah.* Come on, dude, you got this, come up with something intelligent. Ah shit, she just touched his shoulder; it's go time.

The only thing I can think to say comes out, "Hello, Lindsey." And up comes my confident façade because it has to, it's what I do. This is my world and surfer boy needs to go away.

"Michael?" She looks momentarily shocked but then that easy, welcoming Lindsey-smile spreads across her face, and I can tell she is happy to see me. "What the heck are you doing here?"

I can't help but look at the turd with pecs, inconceivably still standing with us, and Lindsey takes notice. "Michael this is Colton, the hotel surf instructor. Colton this is my… this is Michael."

Surf instructor… for the hotel, phew. Relief washes over me, and I am instantly in a better place, but he still needs to go. I can practically still feel his erection from watching her and it's in my way. "Nice to meet you, Colton. Would you mind giving us a moment?"

Lindsey ends the uncomfortable situation for me. "Yes, thanks for the lesson, Colton. I think I've had enough for one day."

Colton seems to get the message and turns professional. "Thanks, Ms. Laverly, if you'd like to continue the lesson later, let me know." He reaches down to pick up the surfboard and slinks away in defeat.

I can't help but smile a little as I turn back to Lindsey.

"Michael." She shrugs and crosses her arms across her amazing bikini covered breasts. "What the heck are you doing in Hawaii?"

My not so carefully thought-out planning sort of ended a minute ago. "Umm." Suddenly I feel the urge to stare at the sand and scratch my head… like that will help. "I need a drink, should we get a drink?"

"Michael, you have a drink." She points to the sweating glass in my hand. "I think I should get a drink." She starts toward the hotel patio, bends over to pick up her clothes, then turns back to me and walks backwards. "You going to follow me?"

I am pulled into motion by the tractor beam that is that smile and that bikini-covered body in motion. I am powerless to resist. "Why stop now?"

CHAPTER 10

*L*indsey

I CANNOT BELIEVE IT. How and why did the man of my dreams, the man of elevator greatness, magically appear in the middle of my dream vacation? I'm suddenly feeling a little ashamed that I ran out of town and disappeared after leaving him in such a state, a little embarrassed for sure. I should have at least emailed him to let him know where I would be, how long I would be gone... something, anything.

Wait.

He is only my boss. I did request my vacation well ahead of the required time with human resources. I followed the rules; I have nothing to feel guilty about.

Yes, Lindsey, but you did almost have sex with the man. Uggh, what to do? What? To? Do?

As I reach the edge of the sand and step onto the concrete patio, my mind is reeling; I am at a loss for where we go from here. And I am feeling very naked. I stop at the first table for two that I come to and pull on my t-shirt before bending over to pull on my shorts while Michael watches every move I make... in complete silence. Great. Why?

"Can I get you two a drink?" Saved by the waiter.

"Yes, I'll have a vodka sour." I glance over at Michael who is staring at me but seems lost in another world. "Michael, do you need anything else?" It doesn't look like he has taken a single drink from the glass in his hand.

He shakes his head and, as a sheepish grin spreads across his face, raises his glass to eye level. "I'm good."

"Shall we sit?" I motion to the second chair. The bistro table for two is a high top black metal version with a ceramic decorative top and a bouquet of fresh flowers in the center. I climb into the chair nearest me, never taking my eyes from his and he is relentless, unwavering in his gaze. I buy some time by reaching back to pull the hair tie from my ponytail and let my hair fall to my shoulders. The tie goes on my wrist for safekeeping and still he stares. "You come all the way to Hawaii to not drink and not talk to me?"

"You look beautiful." He shakes his head as though he is clearing out the cobwebs. "Sorry."

"You never have to apologize for saying that to me."

He raises his beverage and smiles over the edge of the glass before he takes his first drink. "That bikini has me a little out of sorts." As he sets his glass down, he stares at it and shrugs. "Though, to be honest, it may not have been the bikini. You look great."

Wow, I have never seen him like this. He's adorable... but I am still at a loss for what is going on here. "Michael, why are you here? I doubt you came all this way to bring me my planner." An ornery smile spreads across my face; I can't stop myself from teasing him; I love to tease him.

"Thank God for that planner, I only recently stopped needing it."

"You know, Michael, if an erection lasts more than four hours..."

He nods and takes another drink. "You're more powerful than any pill."

"And yet you still haven't answered my question."

"I have to admit, when I saw you with that guy... I thought I would have to beat up a surfer today, *Point Break* style. I came all this way, drove around this whole damn island, sweating my ass off in a shitty rental car and there you were smiling and flirting and on a date."

"Hold on, hold on. I was not flirting and that was not a date."

"Well it looked like it from where I was standing. He sure as heck was flirting with you and then you took off your clothes and you touched him. It took everything I had to contain myself."

"Michael, you're my boss. We've barely spoken outside of work and I've worked with you for two years; heck we've barely spoken at work. You never even look my direction. What are you talking about?"

"But the elevator…" he pauses and I interrupt.

"The elevator was incredible but it should not have happened. I've never done anything like that before and we don't even really know each other."

"I've done nothing but look your way for two years. Not so you would notice but I have, and I want to get to know you better. I feel like I do nothing but look your way at work. I go out of my way just to walk by your office. I think you are incredible, intelligent and beautiful and kind and… I do, I do want to get to know you. I have to, and I came all this way…"

My head is swirling. Did he really just say that? The waiter returns with my drink, and I feel I should dump it over my head instead of drink it just to make sure I am awake and not dreaming. "How did you find me?"

"Opal and some hackers." He nods and takes a drink. "By the way, who shuts off their cell phone for two days anymore?"

Opal? Does that woman know everybody? I am totally confused. I don't remember telling Opal where I was going, and how would a hacker track me if my cell phone is off. "When I'm on vacation, the phone goes off. Wait, did you plant a tracker on me or something?"

"Hmmm... No, but I like where your head is at." An adorable grin spreads across his face. "Opal told me you were in Kauai, and I happen to employ a lot of very smart people; they tracked you to this hotel."

Fucking tech guys. I'll have to kick Alan in the balls when I get back... or give him a giant hug. "How do you know Opal? Isn't she adorable?"

"I just met her, but yes, she is adorable." I look down at the drink in my hands as Michael reaches over and takes my hand in his. A warm tingling sensation runs up my hand and spreads through my chest. "Lindsey, let's get to know each other."

Something is telling me that this all could go horribly wrong, that there are so many reasons why I should just tell him to turn around and go home but I can't help myself. "When do you want to start?"

Michael stands, still holding my hand in his as he stares into my eyes. "I'll get a room and a change of clothes then meet you back here in an hour. We'll have dinner and maybe a walk on the beach?"

"It's a date." I say and turn to walk toward the hotel lobby.

Michael heads to the check-in desk as I float toward my room in a haze of confusion, uncertainty and elation. I can't believe he is here and he came all this way for me. I must be insane and worse, he must be insane. I have a thing for my boss, whom I can't date. And, apparently, he wants me too, but I'm off limits, his employee. And fuck all, he has to be a decent guy, the one guy in the entire world who sticks by his morals and doesn't date employees. And to make matters worse I lied to him, he thinks I'm quitting... because I told him I was. And now I don't know if I can do it. I want to but I'm scared as shit. Quitting means risking everything and nobody will be there to rescue me if I fail. I'll lose the safety of a steady paycheck, invest every dime I've ever made and for what, the chance to lose it all, fall flat on my face and worse, put distance and time between myself and the man who flew halfway across the world, for me.

I can't quit.

I know that if I leave the company and he doesn't see me every day, I'll get busy and he is already crazy busy. Time and distance will take over, to atrophy our connection, our bond, new and tenuous as it is.

And if I don't leave, he can't date me, won't date me.

I am totally screwed.

"Everything okay, miss?" The hotel maid has paused her work down the hall and is watching me as I stand at my hotel room door, staring at the handle as though I don't know how it works. She looks genuinely worried.

"Yes, I'm fine." As I open my door and enter my room I realize what I have to do.

I need Bethany. I need my best friend. I have to call her.

My fingers fly across the keypad of the hotel safe where I've banished my cell phone for the duration of my vacation and it cannot come back to life fast enough. When the screen flashes, an email notification from Luke McKenna pops up on the screen:

Subject: Urgent. Proposal due by end of business Monday.

Shit. That's only forty-eight hours away.

CHAPTER 11

Michael

THE SAND under our feet is still warm from the heat of the day even though the sun is nearing the horizon and the dark of night is beginning to spread across this incredibly beautiful island. In my haste to find her I sped from hotel to spa, spa to luxury resort, I didn't pause to eat let alone take in the beauty of Kauai. The colors, the warmth of the fragrant air, the crackle of a bonfire and laughter of the hotel guests as they ooh and ahh while watching a fire juggler, all combine to erode the stress of mainland life. The orange glow emanating from the distant setting sun is blanketing the green and lush exotic plants growing everywhere. As Lindsey and I head away from the hotel, the laughter becomes distant, muted by the rushing waves that seem to have succumbed to the laidback atmosphere of the evening, still keeping time with the tempo of the receding light but quieter.

Dinner was wonderful, perfect portions to sate the appetite but not overstuff, just like our conversation. Each of us carries a champagne flute wrapped in white linen to collect condensation, our final beverage from dinner. The relaxed island atmosphere is intoxicating, and I am growing euphoric as I glance at her but she has grown quiet and contemplative, gazing over the ocean. The skin of her long neck and bare shoulders glows with the dimming light and her hair flows with each incoming breeze. Her sandals are in her hand, leaving her bare feet to lead up long tan legs that glide in and out the side of her ankle length skirt wrapped around her hips, cut up to her thighs. Her stomach is bare and her amazing breasts are wrapped in a light top that crosses her chest to tie behind her neck.

I want to grab her by the hand, walk with her until I can't take it any longer, let anticipation give way to passion, lay her down in the sand and slowly pull that thin cover away as I work my way down that beautiful body.

But she is keeping her distance, almost purposefully. She is lost in thought.

As though she can feel my stare, she calls over without looking. "Everything okay, Michael?"

"Yes, I'm fine but where have you been?"

"What do you mean?" she asks.

"You were somewhere else. Is there something else going on, something I can help with?"

"Not at all." I can feel her holding back. "I was just enjoying the setting sun."

"Okay then. You kept the conversation light at dinner, which was perfect but now it's time. Tell me about yourself. Who are you, Lindsey Laverly? Where do you come from? Where have you been? Where are you going? What are your hopes and dreams?"

"Wow." She stops walking for a moment. "You really want to get into it."

"We said we were going to get to know each other."

"Okay then you go first." She raises an eyebrow and walks off.

I follow and begin. I don't mind playing this game. I'm easy; my life has been on display for everyone to see, splashed all over the front page of the business section with each new startup, IPO or sale. "I am an open book, almost literally. I've been poked, prodded and examined by every journalist within a thousand miles. What you see is what you get."

"Oh no." She wags her finger at me. "You are not getting off that easy. Tell me about how you grew up, where you grew up, about your family. Why do you do it?"

"Do what?"

"Don't be coy. You know what I mean. All of it."

"Well, I don't mean to bore you to tears, but I

grew up in the ideal American family. Mom and Dad are still married. I am the oldest of four children. I have a younger brother and two younger sisters. Nobody hates each other. We all go home for all the holidays, white picket fence, dog in the front yard, tree house in the back. We weren't rich but we never went without. Mom is a schoolteacher, Dad an engineer. Most of us ended up at ivy league schools including me."

"Wow. Milquetoast Michael. I had no idea. Sounds exciting."

I cannot believe she called me that, though I can't blame her. My life seems almost too ideal, even to me. "Hey, listen. Is that what does it for you? Excitement? Danger? Don't you underestimate me, missy. I am very dangerous. I've been known to eat an entire bowl of popcorn… by myself… and not even floss afterward."

"Oh my. What would you do if you got a kernel stuck in your gums and you didn't know? It could get… it could get… inflamed, Michael. Your life could be in danger."

I stick out my chest and take a deep, exaggerated breath. "I'm willing to risk it. I'm edgy like that."

"Oh and you make billion dollar deals and build massively successful companies."

"That's nothing." I wave her off.

"Yeah, cause everybody does that." She smiles.

"Exactly. Now your turn so I can make fun of you."

"Oh you don't want to hear about my life, you will

want to run for the hills. I may sully your upper middle class upbringing and elite jet-setting status."

I am a little shocked that she is so protective and grows quiet. She seems almost ashamed. Rather than push, I wait and we walk awhile before she starts. "It's safe to say I did not grow up in an ideal American family. We were always just a half step away from trailer trash really. My mom did what she could, but as a high school dropout, she never made much money and we always struggled to buy groceries and keep the power on. But she was a very good mom. She worked two jobs and every dime she made went to my brother and I; she never spent any money on herself. There was only so much she could do, so Jonathan and I spent a lot of time alone, though she always made it known that not going to college wasn't an option. For as long as I can remember, my mom talked about going to college as though it was a given. I was in junior high before I realized that not everyone went to college, so I became the first person in my family to go, first person to graduate."

"And your father?" I ask.

"Never really knew him. He left when I was three, and I never saw him again. I have some cousins out there somewhere, but I don't really know them. All my grandparents are dead, same with my uncles and aunts." She pauses as though she is unsure whether she should continue. "Blue collar work, alcohol and drugs are one and the same with my family, not a combination that leads to long lives. So I learned early to be careful with alcohol; obviously I still drink a little, but I've never touched drugs."

I stop and grab her hand to turn her to me. "That's a good thing, Lindsey."

"Yes, but I've spent my entire life trying to separate my future from my past." She looks down, away from my eyes. "It can get lonely. And most of my family, the ones who loved me, are dead. The rest I had to distance myself from. I couldn't live like that."

I feel the pain in her heart, and I wish I could make it go away; she has had a tough life but has worked hard to lift herself above her circumstances. And she's kind, with an optimistic heart. I can feel it. "Well, I'm here now."

"For about five minutes, Michael. You don't have time for me."

"What are you talking about?" I grab her second hand in mine. "I told you I want to get to know you and I do. I know you are an amazing person, and I'm not going anywhere; you don't need to run from me." I raise a hand to the side of her face and lift her eyes to mine then move my lips to hers and kiss her deeply.

CHAPTER 12

Lindsey

GOOD LORD this man has soft lips and he smells great. Our tongues passionately explore each other's mouths, but all I can think is *what the hell are you doing, Lindsey?* "Hold on a second, Michael. Stop." I take a step back.

All I want is a little time, two seconds to collect myself. It's as though my body thinks we are back in that elevator, finishing what we started. A blazing heat has rushed from my core and down my thighs, so I focus on my breathing. Time to slow things down, reset, because there is no way. This situation is not going down like this. I don't do dark and sad, that's not me. Sure, I didn't exactly have it easy growing up, but I don't dwell on it. But here I am, in the arms of my gorgeous, rich boss, as the sun sets on a beach in paradise, and I am getting a sympathy kiss. No fucking way.

I'm happy, upbeat, good-time Lindsey. This man has to want me because I'm intelligent, beautiful, sexy, funny, and all the other wonderful and amazing things I am. Then we can get down to hot sexy business.

"Is everything okay?" He seems genuinely concerned.

"Yes, I mean no. It can't be like this."

"You want me to stop?" he asks.

"Definitely not. But I don't want you to feel sad or worry for me. I don't need a hero to rescue me. Yes I had a less than ideal family situation but I let it go, made peace with it and moved on. And sure I get lonely from time to time, but that's okay. Who doesn't? For the most part, even back then, I was happy and optimistic. That's just who I am."

"I know that, Lindsey, that's a big part of what attracted me to you." He pauses for a moment. "So we need to flip this thing back around. How do we do that?"

"I could make fun of you again. That always cheers me up."

"Okay, what have you got?" He motions with his hands for me to begin. "Bring it on."

"Were you parents named Ward and June? Did they call you Beaver? Because you kind of look like him."

"Ouch." Michael bursts into laughter and shakes his

head. "That hurts. But yes, my mother vacuumed the house in high heels and pearls."

"I love that."

"The funny thing is, I actually did have a friend named Whitey." He is so serious I don't know if he is telling the truth.

"You did?"

"Nah." He smiles and we continue walking. "I did watch so many re-runs that I used to have nightmares about getting stuck in a coffee cup on a billboard."

"I love those re-runs. I used to stay up so late watching those shows that my mom would get super mad. Did you really have nightmares about that?"

He smiles and shakes his head no. "Should we add gullible to your happy and optimistic list?"

I bump him in the shoulder. "You jerk."

He exaggerates my strength again and stumbles away. Right as I push him, the LED lighting that illuminates the boundary of the hotel's section of beach goes out, and we are left standing in the waning light of the setting sun. "Maybe we should talk about your violent tendencies. I think you have some kind of superpower. You kill electricity."

I don't know how or why the electricity went out, but I definitely take it as a sign. "That's not my superpower." As I move over to him, I take his champagne flute and, together with mine, set them in the sand, then reach around his waist and pull his hips into mine. "I'll show you my superpower."

His mouth is back on mine and my body is flush with heat in an instant. When I feel his cock go hard against my belly, I can't stop the moan that escapes my throat and I press hard against him. I want him naked, to feel his cock in my hand as I grind against him and tease him. This time I'll have his cock inside me, and I know he wants it too. His breathing has become fevered as he thrusts his tongue against mine and runs his hands through my hair.

I stop him before we go too far. I don't want to disappoint him again, but I have to ask because I did not come prepared for him to show up. "Michael." I stop him; he is ravenous, almost incredulous that I'm making him wait.

"Yes, I brought one." He taps his shirt pocket and I attack. I thrust my tongue into his mouth and reach around to grab his right ass cheek to pull him hard into me; when he groans, I melt. I'm so wet I want him to enter me now.

He turns us and pulls me down to lie in the sand with him. As we kiss, his hand moves up to caress my breasts and my nipples are so hard his fingers easily find them through my bandage wrap top. The blue and white top crosses at the center of my chest and wraps around my neck to hold each breast separately. It's sexy and I look good but I wish he would rip it from my body. He doesn't. He's taking his time and driving me crazy; he stops kissing my mouth and rises to hover over me.

"You look so beautiful," he says as he runs his fingers down the outside of the wrap, gently touching my skin and pulling the top in as he moves. I shudder as he crosses over my nipples, exposing them to the night air and he lowers himself to take my right nipple into his mouth. As he flicks it with his tongue I close my eyes, tilt my head back and arch to push my hardened tip further into his mouth. My breathing accelerates, so he stops and I moan louder.

"Don't stop," I gasp.

He seems determined to take his time and I am insane. He lifts himself and his fingers continue their work, the thin fabric slides across my breasts to expose them fully. He guides each side to the center and my breasts roll out as they are freed, the cloth under and between them.

"Why don't you take it off?" I feel like I am begging, and I think he likes it.

"No way. Leave it like this. I like it." He is up and admiring the sight of my freshly exposed skin reflecting the diminishing light. He moves both hands to the top of my chest and glides down over my breasts; my erect, tightened tips rise to meet each finger as they cross over and shudder as they pass. He lowers his mouth to my neglected left nipple to give it the attention it craves then moves to the center of my body just below the gathered material of my top. He inhales to breathe in my scent as he nuzzles my supple belly with his nose and lightly kisses to just beneath my belly button.

Then he rises again to look me over. "I think you chose the perfect outfit. I haven't stopped thinking about how I would get you out of it." He reaches down to find the separation in the flowing sarong I am using for a skirt and raises the material to expose the silk white thong underneath. " I was right, this is the perfect outfit," he continues.

His fingers deftly maneuver through the challenge of unfastening the side of my sarong and I am impressed; even I have a hard time with those buttons. He opens the skirt, spreading it open to each side and moves down to kiss my legs. I spread my knees and roll my hips back so he can access the soft skin on the inside of my thighs. As he crosses over, from one thigh to the next, he stops each time to kiss the outside of the silky thong. I don't know how he does it, but each time his lips land, he is atop my clit pressing harder with each pass. I am writhing in agony at his patience.

As though he knows, he rises up again to admire his work, staring into my eyes. He reaches down and slowly runs his fingers down the side of my thong, pushing the material aside, just like he did my top. When he exposes my wet folds, he slides a finger inside me and I am in bliss as he covers and massages my clit with his thumb, thrusting his finger in and out.

"Michael," I call out.

And then he lies down next to me, never taking his

hand away. He covers the nipple closest to him with his mouth, crosses and covers my chest with his arm so he can work my other nub with his free hand while the other increases its tempo in and out of my opening. It feels as though he is holding me in place with his strong arms, making me even hotter. I roll my hips further, pressing hard into his hand and he lowers his palm so that it presses hard against my clit as he furiously increases the pace in and out, up and down. In mere seconds, I am coming, my insides spasm and clench his finger again and again. This man is an artist and I am breathless in his grasp.

He moves his mouth up to kiss me, but I can wait no longer, so I push him onto his back and cross my leg over to mount him. Now it's my turn. I lean over to kiss him and run my hands up the inside of his shirt to his amazing chest. I take a second to caress his nipples with my fingertips and say, "I've been waiting for this; it's all I could think about since our elevator trip."

I scoot down, open the top button of his shorts and lower the zipper. His underwear is nearly tearing at the seam from his eager cock struggling to free itself. I remove his shorts and boxers, one and all, casting them aside to release his magnificent cock. He closes his eyes and turns his head with a groan as I stroke up and down his shaft with both hands. My how I would dearly love to tease him but I don't. I lower myself and take his full length between my lips. I glide my hot mouth up and down his length, pausing each time to run my tongue around the tip. I move my right hand to massage his testicles and I am shocked. They are swollen to the point of feeling like they may burst at any moment. His shaft is becoming more engorged and harder, if that is possible, but I don't want him to come, not yet. So I stop.

I reach into his pocket to retrieve the condom, and I can't help myself. "Wow," I say. "Have you not… you know… since the elevator."

He opens his eyes and looks at me incredulously. "I've kind of been busy looking for you."

"You poor man." I almost can't believe it. How did he even sleep?

I stare into his eyes, open the condom and place it onto the head of his cock. He is so near the edge it twitches as I roll the latex down the shaft. I love to watch the pleasure he gets from my touch; he never takes his eyes off mine.

I stand and turn away from him to bend over and remove my thong. I stay straight-legged as I bend, then pause for a moment so I can torture him with the view of my ass.

"You are a bad, bad girl," he calls from the sand. "I know what you are doing."

"Are you complaining?" I ask as I kneel over him and take his cock in my hand.

He closes his eyes and turns away again. "No," is all he can muster.

I move the massive head of his cock to my wetness

and begin to feel pressure at my opening as I start to lower myself onto him.

I catch a flash of light out of the corner of my eye just before the LED lights come back to life and now I hear voices drawing near. Many voices and they are moving quickly. I freak out, jump off of him and onto my sarong in a flash, pulling it around me then pulling my top's material back over my breasts.

"No. No. Noooo," Michael calls out in protest. "This is totally not cool. Not again."

By the time he finishes protesting, two families are almost on top of us. "Michael, there are children, you have to cover up."

"Where are my clothes?" He is desperately searching but in my passionate haste I threw them in a nearby bush.

"We don't have time, roll over." I push him over, jump to his opposite side and plop down to block the view of his naked ass. I cover as much of him as I can with my sarong.

"Just what I wanted," he says. "To end up with my dick in the sand."

"Well hello." One of the fathers of the families calls over to us in a slow southern drawl. "Y'all enjoying the evening?"

"Yes, it's beautiful," I respond.

"Wonderful," Michael lifts his head and calls out sarcastically.

"Kids wanted to come down and play so we thought

we'd bring them down for awhile, seein' as how we just got in and all. Hope ya don't mind."

"Not at all, enjoy yourselves," I say, praying they don't notice Michael's shorts in the bush.

As Michael and I watch the two families play, we are both speechless, dumbfounded by our continued bad luck. The longer we have to sit there, the more I think that maybe somebody is trying to tell me something. Maybe this isn't supposed to happen. The passion of sex is wearing off and my head is beginning to clear. I see my entire situation clear and in front of me.

"I can't do this, Michael," I say.

"What do you mean?" he asks.

"I mean maybe this isn't meant to be. Look at the signs. And I work for you. We can't do this."

He looks up at me. "We are doing this, at least trying to. And I thought you quit."

"Well, I did. I mean I'm going to. I think." I don't know what to say to him and need a moment to collect my thoughts. "I'm afraid. I have a great opportunity to leave and start my own firm, but it means risking everything, my job and every penny I own. If I fail, I could lose everything, and I have nothing and nobody to fall back on. But it's my dream, and I'm bidding on a huge job with a very important company, and if I get it, I have to quit which means I will never see you again. But if I don't get it, I will still be working for you which means you can't be with me. We should just end this now."

"Why would you never see me again? We could make it work."

I shake my head. "You know how busy I will be and with how busy you are, there is no way."

"Who is the bid with?" he asks.

"Luke McKenna of Excel Ventures."

"I know them well; they participated in two rounds of funding for my companies. I can put in a good word for you. Let me help you. I'll invest in you."

And then I realize how important it is that I do leave. I have to do this for myself, by myself. I won't have Michael's respect, or respect for myself if I don't try. I can't use his help; it will not be the same, and he can't stop himself from wanting to help, to interfere. I reach over and grab the cloth napkins from under the champagne glasses and use them to cover his naked ass. Then I stand and turn to face him.

"Michael, don't you understand? I don't want your help. I have to do this for me, without a man helping me. Michael, I don't need you to rescue me."

"But why, Lindsey? Listen, everybody needs a little helping hand, even I did. Nobody succeeds alone."

"But I will, Michael. I have to go. They need my bid in less than two days. I have to go back." I hate the thought of leaving him, but I turn and walk away.

"Lindsey, wait," he calls out but can't get up without exposing himself to the two families playing nearby. He may be stuck there for a while, and I use this fact to make my escape. "Damn it. Not again." I hear him say as I walk away.

I will quit my job, and I will get that bid. I am willing to risk everything because I have to. There is no going back now.

CHAPTER 13

Michael

As I pass by the left hand turn I'm supposed to take, the one I make every day that takes me to the office, I almost convince myself that missing the turn was an accident; except I'm a terrible liar, especially to myself. I don't buy it. I know exactly where I'm going, and I can't help myself; it's like she is drawing me in, the thought of catching a glimpse of her is like a tractor beam has ahold of me and won't let go.

It's been two days since she stranded me.

Again.

I was lost in space, powerless to move, paralyzed, while being orbited by screaming tourists. I am still finding sand in the crevasse that is my ass and the creases around the boys. The two hours I laid there before the tourists retreated felt like an eternity. Okay, if I'm being honest, and I always try to be honest with myself, I probably only laid there for thirty minutes. My humiliating sprint to the nearby bushes to retrieve my shorts and the long walk of indignity back to the hotel gave me plenty of time to think about going to her but I didn't. I know… no, I believe, that my best and maybe only chance to have her is to let her go, no matter how painful that is. I know business and I know ambition. I understand exactly what she is going through, and I would be a colossal jackass hypocrite to get in her way.

But I still want to see her, so I slow down as much as I can as I near Get Perky, desperate to catch a glimpse of her through the tinted glass.

And… nothing. Damn. To the office I go and I dare to hope…

But who am I kidding? She's not there, not if she's exactly who I think she is, hope she is, who I know she is.

I park in my usual spot and as I begin my trek across the asphalt, the business portion of my brain takes over. It's as though the parking lot is one long threshold, the crossing of which stills my mind and steadies my breathing. The list begins to form in my head; everything I expect to confront in my morning briefing with Janice. She is one badass assistant, so I prepare for her each day as though she is the enemy.

She can be a formidable foe and if you are not ready… she will whip your ass. And though she never confesses to it, I know she gets a sick and twisted thrill while doing it. The only distraction that keeps interjecting itself into my morning routine is the 'left hand Lindsey detour question'… to do or not to do.

Of course… to do.

As I reach for the door to enter the building, I'm nearly bludgeoned by its leading edge as it passes within an inch of my head, then I deftly dodge the force behind the door, a man rushing by with his nose in his phone.

"Whoa! Slow down, buddy, texting and driving is dangerous." My attempt at covering my irritation with humor is not necessary when I realize who it is.

"Oh, I'm so sorry, Mr. Sinclair." It's Chad, who, of course, would apologetically kiss my ass even if he hadn't almost impaled me with the door. "I didn't see you there."

"Of course you didn't. That would be impossible." I'm trying hard to hide the fact that, because it is Chad, I'm even more irritated. "Where are you off to in such a hurry?"

"Well, you probably know already, but I had no idea she would do such a thing. Very unprofessional." Chad finally stops staring at his phone.

"Who, Chad, who would do such a thing?"

"Well, Lindsey of course. She quit… without notice. And now I have to pick up the pieces."

"Relax, Chad, it wasn't without notice, and I'm sure everything will be fine. We don't have any other events for at least a month." Damn, I was hoping she might work through a two weeks notice, but I'm not surprised. "We have plenty of time to get everything covered."

"Oh, I'm happy to do it, Mr. Sinclair."

"So, why are you leaving, Chad?"

"Oh, I just have to run a quick personal errand, Mr. Sinclair. I'll be back in a jiff, I promise." He nods his head. "Of course, only if you're okay with that."

"Fine, Chad." I turn to head into the building and ignore his bumbling as his voice trails off, heading to the parking lot I presume.

No need to detour left, so I head straight to my office and try not to let the disappointment show on my face. Janice reads me like a book, and I'd rather not face the rack and inquisition.

"Good morning," I say as I pass by her desk and she follows me. She is seated in front of my desk and is sipping her coffee before I have a chance to turn around. "How are you this *wonderful* morning?" I say.

"Now, now." She flashes a half-sympathetic, half-knowing grin my way. "It can't be all that bad. You'll rally. You always do." She is, of course totally put together this morning. A snug blue turtleneck sweater covers the top of her gray knee-length business skirt. She has black leather boots on that rise to… I don't know where because they disappear under the skirt.

Her hair is pulled back in a ponytail and is draped over her shoulder. The faint smell of her 'I conquered this weekend' perfume wafts my way and she looks distinctly confident this morning.

"You have a good weekend?" Like I need to ask.

"None of your business." She reprimands me with her eyes. We both know more about each other than either one of us ever lets on but we always manage to stay professional. "No doubt better than you. Should I have HR begin to search for her replacement?"

"I'm surprised you haven't already." I raise an eyebrow. "But, yes I suppose so. She won't be back."

"Of course I did already." She raises an eyebrow back at me.

"Her weasel assistant is pining for her job already. He almost ran me over in his excitement as he was running out the door on his phone."

"Please." Janice shakes her head and enters something in her tablet. "We do need to talk about him though. But it may involve her. Are you okay with that? I wouldn't want to interfere."

"Yes you would." I pause but she doesn't take the bait. "What's going on?"

"When I heard she quit, I asked if she had turned in her laptop. HR said she left it in her office and that IT had been notified. Well, I just happened to wander that way, and just as I was rounding the corner, I paused long enough to see Chad with her laptop on his desk. I don't know what he was doing but it wasn't good because he slammed it shut when he saw me and hung up on whoever he was talking to. He was excited or nervous enough that he was shaking by the time I passed by."

The little shit. I could fire him just for that. "We need to make sure IT gets that computer sooner rather than later. No telling what he's up to."

"Already done."

"Let's have them dig into it to see if they can figure out what he was doing."

"Already done." She confidently crosses her arms over her tablet and shoots me a 'don't you have something to do' look.

"What else do we have this morning?" I ask.

"Nothing I can't handle."

"Is there any reason I actually need to be here? Why aren't you running this company instead of me?"

Janice rises. "Who says I'm not." She turns to head out the door, and I hear over her shoulder. "And it's because I don't have a penis."

She always tells it like it is… I love this woman. "You're the best." I call out to her.

"Don't I know it," she calls back and closes my office door behind her.

Geez. Could she be more obvious? She's practically a bully. But I pick up the hint and, therefore, my phone. Lindsey answers before the first ring.

"Well, hello there, boss." Oh here we go. She's in a

mood. This should be fun. "Miss me so soon. Is the place falling apart already?"

"Well, I am getting pretty used to you walking out on me, without notice, in the most inopportune moments." Two can play this game. "And don't call me that."

"Oh you're cute. Do you need to borrow my planner again? What should I call you?"

"I'm pretty sure that was company issued so it's my planner now." The sound of her voice and the thought of that planner has me shifting in my seat. "And you can call me... for dinner. Saturday?"

"Well, I'm a bad former employee. I kept the planner; I'm very attached to it. I have quite fond memories of that planner. Do you plan to sue for it?" She pauses but I wait. "And, can't do it. I have a special event I have to go to, mining for clients."

"What's the event? Maybe we can go together, and then we'll be face to face; we can negotiate custody terms."

"I wasn't allowed to date you at work, so you are not allowed to date me at work, and I'll be working."

"Fine, I think I'm getting the message." I pause, wracking my brain for where she could be going, and I see it on the corner of my desk, an invitation to the Hamilton Charity Gala.

I thought I threw that in the trash.

Every big wig in the city will be there; of course that's where she's going. I wasn't planning to attend, I usually just send money but... shit, I think my tux is still at the cleaner's. What is the name of that fucking dry cleaner anyway? "By the way, your chair wasn't even cold yet when we discovered your former assistant feverishly hacking away on your laptop."

"He was probably trying to figure out my password. I very much doubt that simpleton got very far. Does he still have it?"

"No, the IT department has it. We are checking it to see what he was up to."

"You can do that?" she asks.

"To a point, yes, anyone who knows enough can."

"Who cares? I'm very boring. I was all business all the time, so who cares what he sees. I have nothing to hide and my personal email is a different password. He'll never figure that one out."

"You are far from boring, but I figured I would let you know what he was up to. That's why I called."

She bursts into laughter. "Michael, did you forget about asking me out?"

"I don't remember that. I always focus on my victories not my defeats. In fact, as far as I can remember, I've never had any defeats."

"Focus on hanging up. Good-bye, Michael."

"Has anyone ever told you that you have a mean streak?"

"Is that wishful thinking, Michael?" And now her laughter has a decidedly different tone.

"I'm not sure where this is going, and I'm getting scared, so I'm hanging up now."

"Good-bye, Michael."

I get up, march straight to the door and swing it open. "Janice, which cleaner is my tux at?"

"Michael, go back in your office and close the door."

"What? Why? I need my tux."

"Just do it."

So I close the door, and there is my tux hanging on the back of the door, right in front of my face. "Do you have my office wiretapped or my brain," I yell through the closed door.

"You're an open book to me, Michael. I don't need any technological help."

Damn I love this woman.

CHAPTER 14

*L*indsey

I'VE KNOWN of the Hamilton Charity Gala for years, everyone knows of it. Everybody who is anybody, a who's who of power and politics, come together to mingle and gossip every year. And it's strictly invitation only. Thank god for Zach and Bethany. Zach gets invited every year and never attends but because Zach is Zach, he pays for two plates, at a thousand dollars apiece, and considers that good enough. No need to rub elbows with a bunch of stiffs he has little in common with. But rubbin' elbows is just what I need. One client does not a business make. I need these people to know my name and, after tonight when I come calling, at least they will have seen my face. And I am not shy, every big spender will know me before the night is out.

"Are you sure you don't want to come with me," I call to my closet.

"This one or this one. It's got to be one of these two, the rest of your dresses are too slutty." Bethany appears from the depths of my dress rack carrying two dresses. "And I told you I can't. Zach and I have a date tonight."

"Bitch." I'm too nervous to pick one, so I shrug. "You pick."

"Okay, this one." She raises the dress in her left hand, a sleeveless knee length black dress.

"I'll look like a nun, a risqué nun."

"No," she says. "You'll look professional if you accent it with a string of pearls, and you can throw on red heels to let them know you're still dangerous."

"I am dangerous. Aren't I?" I shoot her a pouty look.

"Damn right you are. Grrrr." She twirls and tosses me the dress. "Now get dressed while I pick out a sexy perfume for you, then I can drop you off on my way home."

"I don't need sexy perfume. This is business."

"Sexy perfume is always a must, because... you never know."

"Well, I'm going in under your name, so if I do anything sexy, it's on you."

"Fine," she says as she heads to my dresser. "Just take notes so I know what I did, especially if it's good.

Mmm, hmmm." She makes two thrusts with her hips as she walks.

"And I'm the slutty one?"

"No, just the one with the slutty dresses."

"Takes one to know one," I shoot back. "I can drive myself you know."

"Yes, but this way you can enjoy yourself, and you only have to get a car home. In case you need a little liquid courage throughout the night."

<<>>

Is it weird that I retreat to the bathroom after every interaction with my prey? Come to think of it, is it weird that I think of them as prey? Nah. If I were a man and I had one of my bros in here with me, he'd be amping me up, patting me on the shoulders and saying 'you're killing it, Stallion, now get back out there and knock 'em out', then he'd sing the theme to *Rocky* as he pushed me out the door. But I don't even have someone to tell me if I have lettuce stuck in my teeth, so I retreat to recover, freshen up, reshape this incredibly uncomfortable dress as much as the infrastructure underneath holding me together allows, and give myself a pep talk.

"Okay, Lindsey," I mumble as I apply of fresh coat of

lipstick. "Five solid leads in the bag is good but ten is better. Let's go." And I'm back out the door. 'Ba ba bum ba dum, da da dum da dum', go get 'em, Rock.

As I near the end of the bathroom entryway and start to cross the grand hall that leads to the ballroom, I can hear the band already. No DJ tonight, this is a classy event and a glance up at the ceiling reminds me where I am; the only hotel in town large enough and swanky enough to handle an event like this. The ceiling is decorated like a European cathedral and they pump in that smell that tells you, if you want to stay here... never mind you can't afford it.

Today they might laugh me out the door but some day this place will be begging me for my business.

It takes a minute for my eyes to adjust to the darkened ballroom, so I stand just past the entrance and scan the immediate area for my next victim. I heard Jack Simons is somewhere in here, but I haven't spotted him yet. He heads a non-profit charity, primarily funded from his own fortune, and sponsors about a dozen events throughout the year. I would love to have his business. Where are you, Jack, you lucky man, you're dying to meet me. I don't actually know what he looks like but I hear he's hot. I mean, I'm not looking, nor do I want to be another notch on his belt, but a little eye candy is not a deal killer. His reputation with women is not great, he's supposedly a bit of a man-whore, but I've only heard rumors.

Out of the corner of my eye, a young-ish stud is

making a beeline straight for me. Oh, buddy, I hate to disappoint you but you are barking up the wrong nun.

"Hello there, you look a little lost and a little lonely. Can I accompany you to the dance floor? I'd love to help with that serious look on your face; let's replace it with a smile." He puts out his hand. "My name is Jack, I'm one of the sponsors of the event tonight, and I don't believe we've met."

Surely this is just coincidence. "Jack..." I ask.

"Jack Simons."

"Jack Simons. I was just looking for you."

I smile and shake his hand.

"Well, thank goodness you found me." He asks with a worried look on his face, "Do we know each other?"

"I am Lindsey Laverly with Superior Events and Occasions. I just wanted you to be able to put a face to my name so that when I come to win your business, we will already be familiar. And I don't mean to be conducting business on such a beautiful night, but a girl's got to take her shots when she can."

"Hmmm." He crosses his arms and puts his hand to his chin. "Well, relax, Lindsey Laverly, everybody here is conducting business. But for now, let's dance." He puts out his hand again. "Since now I know your face."

I take his hand and follow him to the dance floor where, of course, a slow dance is playing. Before I prep my opening line he spins me, pulls me in and we are close enough that I already know the flavor of mouthwash he uses.

"I thought I knew everybody who received an invitation." Looking me up and down from just inches away would seem impossible but somehow he does it. "But I don't know you."

"Zach and Bethany Steal donated but couldn't make it so they offered me their invitation." I arch my back to try to put some distance between us.

"Bullshit."

"Excuse me."

He shakes his head and smiles. "I said bullshit. Zach always receives an invitation even though everyone knows there is no way he will come. We only continue to send him an invitation because he never fails to donate, but I know Zach; he tries to stay as far away from these kinds of things as possible. So, now, would you like to revise your story?" His hand slides down my back. "Cause I'm not going to kick you out."

"You seem to know so much. Why don't you tell me why I'm here?" I glance around the dance floor to try and deflect his stare.

"I've been watching you troll for clients all night. The only thing more obvious than your ambition is your beauty, and if I didn't have to mingle so much, I would have had you wrapped in my arms an hour ago." Of course his hand slides a little further down, now nearing the curve of my ass.

"Good. Except you underestimate my ambition." I push back for real this time to gain some separation. "I'm all business tonight."

"Jack." A deep but familiar voice calls from behind. "You look like you need to be rescued. Mind if I cut in?"

"Mikey." He releases me then steps back. "Of course. Do you two know each other?"

"Lindsey used to work for me." Michael shakes Jack's hand but has not looked my way yet. "She's the best event planner I've ever worked with. You should really think about hiring her to handle your events."

"Well, we've only just met but I'm sure she's very talented." He bows and begins his retreat. "You two enjoy the dance."

In an instant, I am in Michael's arms but somehow he still has managed to not look at me. "Well, hello there, I did not expect to see you here," I say to break the ice.

He finally looks me in the eye, but only for a moment. "It seems I am continually rescuing you from the clutches of another man."

"Is that the reason for the deep manly voice? Sending signals to warn off the young stud." I can't help but smile. "Are you claiming your territory, Mikey is it?"

"What are you talking about?" He is scanning the room and turning me whatever direction he wants to look. "And don't ever call me that if you expect me to respond."

"You're doing it now. Are you still looking for him?" I stop the spinning and shake him until he looks me in the eye. Then I lower my voice as much as I can. "Cause I think he's gone, *Mikey.*"

He sighs and finally smiles at me. "Listen, Batman, I can't be held responsible for what happens when my inner beast takes over."

"Do I need to give you a minute to pee on all four corners of the dance floor?"

"Well, I did that before I cut in… but you're probably right, since he was just here I should probably do it again." He steps back and starts unzipping his pants.

"Uggh. Gross. You are an animal." I grab him as he feigns that he is walking away. "Get back here before you get me kicked out."

"Whatever it takes to get you to stop using that ridiculous voice. And I said beast, not animal. It's important that you know the difference."

"Well, I would like to but for some reason you can't seem to ummm… shall we say, seal the deal."

"Oh, really." He pulls me in close and we pick up the beat of the music. "You talk a pretty big game for someone who keeps running away."

"Oh, I definitely didn't run, but one mustn't ignore the signs." I waggle my fingers in front of his face. "Bad juju."

"You're nutty."

"True." I shrug. "Yet you just keep following me. By the way… why are you here?"

"Well, I thought you could use some help. I know

most of these people; thought I could introduce you to a few of them, if you want."

"Michael, if I rely on you to introduce me, the only person they are going to see is you. You cast a pretty large shadow. And I never told you where I was going tonight. How did you even know I would be here? Did you imbed a GPS tracker in me?" I look up and down my wrists.

"Me? Nah. As you may have noticed, I haven't been able to imbed anything in you… yet. And are you sure? I really feel like I can help."

"Absolutely not." I stop us, step back and take his hands in mine. "I love that you came here just for me. You are adorable, but like I told you, I have to do this myself. Now… we can sit down for a minute and have a drink, then you must leave. I'll get us some drinks; you find us a table."

"Okay, but don't go far." He pulls out his phone and fakes a look at it. "My GPS signal in here is pretty weak."

I head one direction and he goes the other. Thankfully, the line at the bar is only two deep, so within five minutes I am circumventing the perimeter of the dance floor in search of Michael… and I don't see him anywhere. As I reach the last table and perform a U-turn for another pass through the tables, I walk a little slower this time. When I pass by a very tall woman with six-inch black heels and a skin-tight, very short black dress, I hear my name.

"Lindsey." No wonder I didn't see him, he was camouflaged in long legs and ass. Guess she didn't get the slutty dress memo. "Here she is. Julie, I'd like you to meet Lindsey." Michael stands and motions between the two of us. "Lindsey, Julie."

I hand Michael his drink and set mine down so I can shake her hand. As I turn back around, I can't help myself. My eyes start low and follow her toned legs with light brown skin up to her long, jet black hair, pause at her smiling full lips and rise to meet dark brown eyes. "Wow, you're gorgeous." I smile and find her hand.

"Aren't you a doll to say so?" She brought along her sultry voice to match the dress. I'm fucking Batman here. Obviously she's not wise to this fact yet. "But not gorgeous enough for Michael. He broke my heart, and I still don't think I'm over it. We used to date you know, in case he hasn't told you."

"Oh, we're not together." I stammer and squeak as I reach for my drink. *Shit I can't be Robin, pull yourself together, girl.*

"Does Michael know this?" She turns and smiles at him.

"I seem to remember things a little differently." Michael takes a sip of his drink. "But you are still a troublemaker."

"Well, darling, this *is* my troublemaker dress." She moves her hands to her sides and slides them down, along the curves of her micro outfit. "Michael tells me you'll be working with Luke, he's an absolute doll, his office is just across the hall from mine."

"You work at Excel Ventures?"

"Five glorious years now. That's how I met Michael."

"Well, maybe I'll see you there. I'm hoping to find out if I have the winning bid soon." I cross my fingers.

"You are Superior Events and Occasions, right?" she asks.

"Yes."

"Well, darling, I heard you got it, that it was a done deal."

"Oh, well that sounds great. I haven't heard from Luke in a while, maybe I need to check my email, no place for a phone in this dress."

"Tell me about it, darling. And I think it's time to take the power of my troublemaking somewhere it'll do me some good. Lindsey, it was a pleasure to meet you." She looks both Michael and I up and down and points at both of us. "If there is anything I can do for you two, please let me know."

As soon as she is out of earshot I turn and smile at Michael. "So you two used to date?"

"Not really."

"And *you* broke *her* heart?"

"No, not really."

"She's seems as though she doesn't want to be done with you. Or, now that I think about it, both of us."

"She's unique, quite a handful."

"Oh, there is more than a handful there."

He reaches up and loosens his tie. "Should I go now?"

"Probably."

"Thanks for the beverage." He gulps the rest of his drink and sets it down. "Mind if I track you down again, maybe… tomorrow?"

"Not sure I have a choice."

"Don't stay out too late, I'll know." He kisses me on the cheek and heads for the exit. "You smell amazing by the way."

CHAPTER 15

Michael

How long do I have to wait before I text her? I press send and my text goes out to Janice. It's 8:30 on a Sunday morning and she'll be pissed, but she's used to me calling her at all hours of the day and night. I have no doubt she was up late last night, but I know she will reply, unlike Lindsey who, unfortunately, I do not have a tracker on and, therefore, have no idea how late she stayed at the gala.

Who are we talking about? And do you know what time it is? What day it is? Janice's reply comes almost immediately after I press send.

You know who we're talking about, and of course I know what time it is. I waited two hours to text you. You should thank me. I didn't sleep for shit last night, tossing and turning, thinking of Lindsey.

Oh, I will thank you when I make you pay for this. Janice pauses before sending the next line. She is fake fuming for me because she knows I love to annoy her. *Stop bothering me and start bothering her. I'm sure it's late enough.*

Thanks, you can go back to sleep now. Nervous smiley face emoji sent.

Who says we were asleep. Horny devil face emoji.

Message received, and TMI.

I feel like maybe I should give Lindsey a little more time. I'm sure she's still asleep and doesn't want to be bothered, so I pace, heavy-footed, doing laps around my kitchen island. When I need to think, I often find myself moving in time to the rhythm of the echo of my own steps as they reflect back at me through the sparse décor of my bachelor pad. Most of the time, I'm not aware that I'm moving and look over my shoulder, surprised I haven't worn a path in the flooring. I'm not hungry but I mindlessly open the refrigerator door, looking for... nothing. It's basically empty except for a few bottles of ancient salad dressings and a jar of blackberry jam. I'm not much of a chef and don't have anyone to cook for anyway. The refrigerator door rattles as I slam it shut and survey the artificial and sparse décor that is the interior of my house. The plants and decorations look like they belong in a model home and have nothing to do with me, my likes or my personality. I paid an interior decorator when I bought the place and haven't changed a thing since I told her to do whatever she wanted and she did, which turned out to be as little as possible. Oh well, who gives a damn; I am rarely here, except to sleep.

To hell with this, I have to see her again. I haven't stopped thinking of her since the elevator. It's like she has me in a trance. *You ready?* I enter the text for Lindsey and press send, then I wait... and wait, and head to the coffeemaker for my fourth cup of coffee when I hear my phone buzz.

For what? Lindsey replies.

Our date.

We have a date? Did I miss something last night? She asks.

This is me tracking you down, and it is now officially tomorrow.

Not sure that is ever true, but okay. What are we doing? Is she texting philosophical, this early in the morning, on a Sunday?

I send back. *It's supposed to be a nice day, how about a morning hike? Big Bears Lake? And a picnic.*

A hike? Uh oh. Sounds like she may not be much of a hiker.

You do hike? Right? I ask.

Oh... yeah. Like, all the time. I'm a regular up there. Lindsey the hiker they call me.

Who is they?

This time she takes a while to respond. *The big bears... duh!*

Great. Shall we meet at the trailhead, say 10:30?

Sure. She replies. *What's a trailhead?*

Oh boy, this should be interesting.

I ARRIVE at the trailhead early and spend some time stretching and placing the lunch I prepared into my pack. The parking lot for the trail is right on the edge of town and not hard to find, so I am fairly confident Lindsey can manage to find me. I come here all the time, especially this time of the year, to be alone, decompress, and get a little exercise, but I have a feeling that, until today, Lindsey had no idea this place existed. I half expect her to arrive at least twenty minutes late, but just as the thought crosses my mind, a white Toyota Camry barrels into the parking lot and screeches to a halt next to my Four Runner.

I make it to the driver door just as it swings open and Lindsey's smiling face pops out of the car. "You made it," I say.

"Did you think I'd get lost? I told you I come here all the time." She smiles and glances down at the largest pair of hiking boots I've ever seen. She taps the toes of them together. "You like them?"

"You're adorable," I say to her because I just can't help myself.

"What? I mean yes I am, but why?"

"You've never hiked a day in your life."

"What do you mean?" She lifts one of her giant boots. I didn't even think they made this type of boot anymore. We used to call them waffle stompers when we were kids because of the pattern they make in the snow with each step. They are big, stiff, light brown leather boots with red laces and a massively heavy sole. "You see these things? These are hiking boots."

"Where did you get those?" I ask.

"My neighbor Penny loaned them to me. They were a gift but she never wore them, so she said I can have them."

"A gift from the seventies? You can't wear those, you'll have a blister before we make the first turn." I have to cover my mouth to keep from bursting into laughter, and also because she is so damn cute. "Please tell me you brought your sneakers?"

"Of course, you think I want to wear these the rest of the day? Don't I need the ankle support? Look at these things, nothing is moving in these babies."

"Exactly," I say. "And grab a jacket."

"A jacket?" she asks sheepishly. "It's pretty warm out."

"Forget it, I brought you one. You'll be thanking me as we head up the trail and get in the trees. It is still winter after all." I can't help but smile at her. "You've never been here, have you?"

"Awww, the big, strong outdoorsman is taking care of me." A guilty giggle escapes before she can stop herself. "I've probable driven by this place a thousand times and had no idea it was here."

As she dives into her car to change into her sneakers I ask, "Been to the gym lately?"

"Who's Jim?" she calls back.

"I guess we'll take it slow."

But she does remarkably well on the trail, and I let her lead the way. She must be in decent shape because she keeps up a good pace and manages to talk the whole way, agog with the beauty of the trail and trees, positing how she could possibly have lived here as long as she has and never been up here.

"So how goes the big new contract? Have you been busily signing contracts and getting things organized?" I ask.

"Okay, I guess." She turns her head to respond to me as we make the next switchback and nearly trips over a tree root.

"Careful. Eyes front." I laugh. "Why do you guess?"

"Well, your girlfriend—"

"Ex."

"Mmm hmm. Ex-girlfriend said she thought I had the contract, but I haven't heard for sure. I've been emailing Luke all week and didn't hear back from him. I'm sure he's just been busy. Anyway, I have a meeting tomorrow to negotiate for the space. I don't want to risk the chance that it gets booked by someone else. That hotel is always… " She's turned the final corner, catching sight of the lake as it peeks through the trees, and for the first time all day she is speechless. When we clear the trees, she continues walking until we reach a ridge overlooking the entire lake.

"What do you think?" I ask as I walk up beside her.

She takes a long moment to respond before shaking her head and exhaling. "It's the most beautiful thing I've ever seen." She wipes a tear from her eye.

A silent morning mist lingers over the stoic and still water, flat as glass, only periodically interrupted by a trout touching the surface. The magical scent of the cool water mixed with the pine of the trees fills the air. A small flock of birds breaks the silence and squawks to life as an eagle launches from a nest high in a tree across the lake. The majestic and massive bird glides across the surface of the water, his white head scanning the depths, its flight effortless and unconcerned, as though he might make the effort for a meal but is content not to.

I take her hand in mine as we take in the grandeur before us, silently in awe. She moves closer, and I wrap her in my arms.

"Thanks for bringing me here," she whispers.

"I love this place and I wanted you to see it." And I realize, I don't think I've ever felt this way about anyone before. Lindsey is the first woman, the first person, I have ever brought here. This is where I come to center myself and now she is in my center.

"Hungry?" I ask.

"Famished."

I point to the high side of the lake. "See that pointed boulder hanging over the inlet? It's a great place for a picnic."

She takes the lead again and we follow the undulating trail that circles the lake, ducking through bushes and climbing over fallen tree trunks until we reach the boulder. I put down my pack and join her at the edge of the giant rock that points like an arrow to the natural dam at the opposite shore.

And she turns to face me. "What exactly is going on here?"

"We're about to have a picnic." I say. "Though not much of one. The only food I could find in my house is peanut butter, blackberry jam and tortilla chips."

"You know what I mean, Michael."

I reach out and take her hands in mine. "Well, I love this place, and I had to see you again so I thought, or hoped, you would love it too."

"I do love it, but what are your intentions? I need to know because I'm really exposed right now, trying to make serious changes in my life, I can't take this if you just want to play around." She takes her hands away and faces the lake.

"Hey." I grab her shoulder and turn her back around, but she only stares at the ground. "Look at me. Don't you know, can't you tell?"

"What?" she asks, but still won't look at me.

"I've fallen for you. I followed you halfway around the world and back again. Dressed up in a penguin suit, pleaded with you to let me help you." I put my finger under her chin and lift her gaze to mine. "I've fallen in love with you."

"How do you know, Michael? You could just be lusting for something you haven't been able to have yet. You barely know me."

"You're damn right I lust after you but don't think I don't know you. I know that you like to seem like the carefree, funny, party girl but you're not. You are very intelligent and serious about the right things, with big plans for yourself, and you're kind and generous."

"Am not."

"You don't think I notice that you donate the most, out of all the employees, to the children's fund every year, even though most of the employees make more money than you."

She frowns and furrows her brow. "We should talk about that."

"Stop."

"Well, you said I wasn't funny." She shrugs.

"I have not been able to keep my eyes off you since you started working at the company. I go out of my way and walk down your aisle every chance I get. I watch you all the time, have to see you every chance I get." Listening to myself, I pause. "Am I sounding a little stalker-ish?"

"Yes, but keep going. I've never had a stalker before."

"I know you never say a bad word about anybody,

even when you could, even when you should. Everybody likes you, even Janice."

Her eyes open wide. "Janice likes me?"

"Yep," I say as I nod my head in assurance.

"How do you know? Did she say something?"

"No, but she knows about me and you and she hasn't tried to stop me. She even had my tux ready for me so I could go to the gala.

"Wow." She nods with me. "She does like me. The Janice seal of approval."

"The highest honor a civilian can earn." We both pause in recognition of the moment. "But what about you?" I ask. "I just told you I am falling in love with you, and you're still making jokes."

"I'm sorry, I kinda get worse the more nervous I get." She releases my hands and reaches around my waist to pull me to her. "Well, you're not the only one who's been doing the watching. I've had a crush on you since my first day at the office. I've thought about you and dreamt about you more times than I want to admit. I know just about everything there is to know about you, but if all I ever knew was that every employee who works for you loves you, that would be enough. You're a super business stud and way too sexy for your own good." She pauses and looks into my eyes. "And, Michael."

"Yes?"

"I'm falling in love with you too."

She closes her eyes and we share a kiss, our first

real kiss. When her lips touch mine, a shockwave emanates from the top of my head, radiates through me, down the back of my skull, through my belly, and down to my toes. The wave warms my entire body as it moves through me, and I am sure this is it. She is it. Then, as we finish, she smiles, buries her head in my chest and squeezes me tight.

But I just can't help myself. "So, you've dreamt about me huh?"

And without missing a beat she says, "How'd you know blackberry jam is my favorite?"

CHAPTER 16

Lindsey

I DIDN'T EXPECT to be back in the Amsterdam Hotel this soon but I have to say I'm very excited that I am, and even more nervous. This represents a huge commitment for me. I'm not sure what kind of a deposit they will require but I know it can't exceed ten thousand dollars… because that's all I have. As I near the front entrance, my heart is pounding in my chest, so I pause and take a few deep breaths.

I say to myself, "Okay, Lindsey, you got this. You said that one day they would be begging you for my business and that starts today." I jump into the circulating door and take baby steps until the opening appears and it's chest out, full stride forward, across the lobby toward the administrative offices. I cross the lobby diagonally for no real reason; I have plenty of time, so I slow down, close my eyes and run my hand across the soft leather back of the couches of the center seating area. I love the feel and smell of real Italian leather, and I'm calmer already.

"Oh, hi, Lindsey." Before I even open my eyes I recognize the voice. It's Chad, coming from the direction of the back offices.

"Hello, Chad." I'm a little stunned, so I just blurt it out, "What are you doing here?"

"Good to see you too," he says with a smug little grin. "Heard you started a new business venture. How's that going?"

"Where did you hear that?" Then, for some reason, I try to remember I have manners. "Sorry, never mind. Things are going well."

"That's great, I'm sure you'll be fine… taking a big risk and all, quitting your job without even a single client lined up."

There's no sense in worrying about what Chad thinks he knows, so I let it go. "And, what brings you here?"

"Just taking care of some business." He puts his hand on my shoulder and looks down his nose at me, straight into my eyes. "I have to run now, you have no idea how busy I am."

Something has definitely changed. Chad has never

looked me straight in the eye, not once in two years. "Bye, Chad."

It's so strange to see him here, today of all days. The simpering underling is gone, replaced by a cocky dickhead, suddenly full of himself; must have been promoted into my job. But who cares? I can't worry about that now because I have bigger fish to fry today, so I continue to the receptionist desk. "Hi, I'm Lindsey Laverly. I have an appointment with Diane Bunton.

"Hi, Lindsey, have a seat, Diane will be right with you." The receptionist smiles and points me in the direction of a nearby couch. "Can I get you a water?"

"No, thank you," I respond and head to the couch.

As I turn and prepare to sit, a voice calls from behind, "Lindsey?"

"Yes."

"Hi, I'm Diane. Nice to meet you, come on in." She shakes my hand and I follow her to her office. "Have a seat."

"Thank you." I put my bag on the floor next to me and sit.

"What can I do for you today?"

"I'm an event planner and I have a very important client who has an event coming up. I'd like to discuss reserving a space."

"How much space do you need and do you have an idea on the date?" She turns to her computer monitor and opens her scheduling program.

"Well, it's a big event so we would need the main

ballroom for the weekend of March twenty-third." I open my planner and pull out a pen.

A disappointed look comes over her face and my heart sinks. "Oh, I'm so sorry. I literally just booked those dates about five minutes ago, terrible timing I'm afraid."

"You're kidding." I want to cry.

"No, I'm sorry. Would another date work?"

"No."

"I always try to help in any way possible, even it means we lose your business. Perhaps I can recommend another location? I know most of the hotel managers in the area." She is sincere but all I can hear is a continuation of the alarm bells going off in my head that started when I saw Chad.

"To Chad?"

"Excuse me?"

"Was it Chad? Did you book it for Chad?" I ask.

"You know Mr. Dixon?" She nods.

"Who is the client?" It's got to be Michael, and I might be able to get him to get him to choose a different hotel.

"I'm afraid I can't divulge that information."

"I can give you a $10,000.00 deposit." The desperation in my voice is embarrassing, but I can't help myself.

"I'm sorry, but we require a $20,000.00, non-refundable deposit, which Mr. Dixon paid when we signed the contract." She sits back in her seat, crosses her arms and I get the message.

What the fuck is going on here? How did this happen to me? "Thank you for your time." I shake her hand and am out of her office before she can finish apologizing. If that weasel is heading back to the office, and I hurry, I might be able to catch him before he heads inside. But I've got to text Michael first so I stop, sit down on the lobby sofa and whip out my phone. I know if I ask Michael for help, he won't let me down.

As I furiously type, I'm confused by the sound of Michael's voice from afar. I look up and there he is, there they are, Michael and Julie, waiting for the elevator. The doors open, she hooks her arm in his, giggles like a she-whore, and whisks him away, leaving nothing behind but a trail of legs and ass.

I am speechless.

What the hell did I just see?

Did the man who just confessed to falling in love with me disappear into the bowels of a luxury hotel with his supposed ex-girlfriend? Could this day get any worse? Did I just lose my only contract, and Michael, in the span of five minutes?

I don't know what to do. So I just sit with my jaw on the floor.

My heart is shattering in my chest, and the shock of millions of pieces falling to the pit of my stomach has stolen my breath, but I cannot, no, will not, chase after any man who would do such a thing. If that is the way he wants to be, he can have her; they can have each other.

A cool rush of tears rolls down my cheeks, but I refuse to go down without a fight. I need to save my future, my business, and I can't sprint out the door fast enough.

As I drive toward the office, I run every stop sign and speed as fast as I can, but I hit the red light at First Street. I am raging and crying, and crying and raging when I get a text… from Michael.

"Bad news, Lindsey." Duh. Michael, you have no fucking idea. "Found out that Chad got into your email before we got to your computer. You may want to change your passwords. We are trying to figure out what he was doing but are not having much luck. Sorry."

I push my car to its limits after the light changes. My tires squeal as I make the turn into the office parking lot and I see him. The weasel is almost to the back entrance, so I screech to a stop at the curb and jump out. "Chad," I yell.

"Lindsey." He smiles and heads my way. "I take it you just finished up at the hotel. Bad news?"

"What the fuck are you up to, Chad?"

"Not sure what you mean, Lindsey." He smiles and feigns concern. "Have you been crying?"

"You know what I mean, Chad. What are you up to? I need that space and you stole it from right under my nose."

"Now, now, Lindsey, I would never do such a thing." He shoots me his best innocent look, but I have been wise to his bullshit for a long time.

"Is it for Michael?"

"For who?"

I have to restrain myself from smacking his coy look off his face. "Don't fuck with me, Chad, I'll have your job for this."

"Oh, it's yours, sweetie. Please… I'm sure Michael will give you your job back. Though you may have to stop fucking each other. That's against company policy." He pauses while that last sentence hangs in the air before he smiles. "I was just going in to clean out my desk. You see I've started my own business."

All the air escapes from my lungs and I am frozen. Suddenly the lack of communication from Luke no longer feels inconsequential.

"Why that space… on that weekend?"

He pushes his chest out and steps forward to get in my face. "Oh, you know why. Don't you, Lindsey?" He's leering over me now. "You don't think I'd let you get the better of me, do you? Your business is now my business, your contract is now my contract."

"Bullshit, I'll tell them what you're up to. Michael will vouch for me. They'll never stick with you."

Chad laughs in my face. "Oh, I don't think so. They committed to our company, Superior Events and Occasion Inc., over company email. You know, I love the name we came up with. I think I'll keep it. Of course, I own the business registration, I personally locked down the hotel reservation, and I've even posted the good news to the company website. Everything is signed, sealed and delivered." He flashes what looks like a press release on his phone. "By the way, Luke understands and wishes you the best as you deal with your personal issues. The announcement of your resignation from the company, just went out."

My head is spinning, and all I can think to say is, "Michael knows you've been in my email. You really think you can get away with this?"

"It's a done deal, sweetheart, and your boyfriend won't do a damn thing. I've fucked up your world; you don't want me to fuck up his too, do you? You want to be responsible for that?"

"You're bluffing, you don't have the balls."

"Sweet Lindsey. One step behind and clueless again." He is reeking of shit-eating smugness. "I have proof of everything you two have been up to, including this." He swipes across his phone and opens a photo. It's me on top of Michael, half-naked, on the beach in Hawaii. "You really think he is willing to risk his IPO over a scandal with an employee, over you? I wouldn't bet on it. No, I think you should slink back to your shitty apartment and start searching the want ads for a job or I go public with this. Of course, you could ask for this job back I suppose, though it may result in a lot less sex on the beach."

I have never seen Chad this way. He has the look of

a killer. Gone is the sniveling pussy. "Why, Chad?" I have to ask. "I treated you well. I was always nice to you."

"You think I kissed your ass for two years just to see you go off and become a success before me, to beat me?" He shakes his head at me and sneers. "You're a naïve fucking woman. You should be thanking me. I'm saving you from massive failure and embarrassment. And if you think Michael wants to be with a loser, you're even more gullible than I thought. I tell you what… I'll do you a solid and not let him know I kicked your ass. If you don't tell him, he may never know, and maybe he'll keep you around for awhile."

Fury is rising within my body, turning me into a shaking mess, and I can't help that I may burst into tears any second. "You're a fucking asshole." It's all I can think to say.

"Good. You've learned a powerful business lesson." He turns to head into the office but makes a shooing motion first. "Now… run along."

As he disappears through the door, I am sobbing and shaking so bad that I barely make it back to my car and collapse into the driver seat.

CHAPTER 17

Lindsey

Knock, knock, knock.

"Go away," I yell from beneath the mountain of blankets that is my fortress of solitude. My grandmother's afghan is layer two and whenever it's been called on, it has acted as an impenetrable force that has kept me safe for years. I've never been lied to, cheated, or betrayed from behind its enchanted defenses.

Knock, knock, knock.

"I said go away." Louder this time. I've lost track of time and have no idea how long it's been, but I feel that I may never get out of bed again. The salty, streaked remains of tears are crusted along the sides of my face and, though I'm not sure, snot has likely covered the rest. I covered my bathroom mirror for when I'm forced to use the toilet. I may never look myself in the face again.

Knock, knock, knock.

"Fine." I'm going to kill this person but it better not be Michael because he will have to wait. I can't kill him looking like this.

I pull my legs into my chest, kick the mountain of covers off and stomp to my front door. Upon peering through the peephole, I can only see the back of a female figure. At least it's not him.

I swing the door open and yell, "What?"

"Good lord, it's worse than I thought." She is fully made up and looking like a million bucks, as usual.

"Janice?" I turn, head back toward my fortress. "What do you want?"

"Oh no you don't." She grabs me by the arm and turns me toward my bathroom. It's as though she knows that if I make it back beneath my fortress, I cannot be touched and may be irretrievably lost for eternity.

"Did he send you?" I ask just as she pulls the towel off my mirror and I cringe at the horror.

"Who? Michael?"

Turning to face her, I put up a finger. "Please don't say that word."

She moves her hand in front of her face to ward off the wretched odor that is my halitosis. I'm pretty sure I made her eyes water, but I look away before I can tell, to admire my pathetic condition in the glass that does not lie.

"We need to talk, but not here." After running water over a washcloth, she goes to work on my cheeks and continues, "We have to get you out of here. This place smells like a bag lady's coffin if she was buried for years with two moldy cats."

"Aren't you a dear for saying so." A chorus of bass drums begins to pound in my head and I am in pain. "Owww." I reach for my temples but they hurt too much to touch.

"You need coffee."

The maximum state of dress I relent to is a hoodie and a pair of sweatpants that could easily be mistaken for pajamas, which suits me just fine. Before I know it we're three-quarters of the way into our journey and Get Perky is within sight. It may be my imagination but I think I can smell it already.

I really do need coffee.

When Janice opens the door, my brain is immediately awash in the welcoming balm that is coffee aroma. If it had arms, it would be racing forward for a deep embrace with its love. I feel better already.

Janice heads to the counter and says, "Get us a table, I will get our drinks. What do you want?"

"Just tell Chris it's for me, he knows what I like." I turn to the seating area and am immediately greeted with a welcoming smile I know well.

"Hello, Opal." The recognition that I am smiling is

amplified because the feeling has become foreign over the last few days.

"Well hello there, dear. How are you?"

"Oomph." I shrug. "A little rough lately."

"Well sit down, let's talk about it." She motions to the seat at her left.

"You don't mind?"

"Of course not." Today must be blue day because she is dressed from head to toe in the brightest version of blue ever seen in a sunlit sky. I have no idea how she looks so well put together each time I see her. She's wearing bright blue heels and a knee-length skirt with a matching jacket covering a silky white blouse barely peeking through at her neck. Her usual bright red lipstick and nail polish contrast perfectly to match the rose of her cheeks and her perfectly applied makeup. From head to toe, makeup to clothes, there is not a wrinkle on this woman, like she was lifted from a magazine cover of the 1950s. Her matching blue gloves, purse and hat sit on a chair behind her. "Should we wait for your friend?"

"To be honest, Opal, I'm not sure. Janice and I are not really friends; she works for Michael."

"Your beau."

"Long story." I sigh. "She came to my apartment and dragged me here. I'm not really sure what's going on."

"Oh, I think I have a pretty good idea but let's find out together. What do you say?" She smiles, takes a long sip of her coffee and watches over the rim of her cup as Janice approaches. "Hi, Janice, my name is Opal." Opal reaches out and shakes Janice's hand. "I hope you don't mind, I asked Lindsey if the two of you would join me."

"Not at all." Janice smiles at Opal as though she has known her forever, takes the seat across from her and hands me my drink. "Something tells me this conversation just got infinitely better."

I see that Janice has a collection of scones and pastries, and I suddenly realize that I am starving. "Is one of those for me?" I ask.

"That guy at the counter just started giving me stuff. Not sure why, but he just kept staring and handing me all this. I didn't even pay for them so, yes, have whatever you want." She pushes the bag full of goodies across the table.

As I begin stuffing my face with a chocolate filled scone, Opal's smile widens and she says, "Isn't he adorable? He always treats us so well."

I practically spray crumbs and powdered sugar everywhere as I mumble with my mouth full, "That's Chris." I take a moment to swallow and grab a sip of coffee. "He must like you though, I usually have to trick him for extra stuff."

Janice looks back at Chris who, I just notice, hasn't taken his eyes off her. Then she turns back to face me with a devilish grin on her face. "Chris huh? He is very cute. Very young but very cute."

"Okay, girls, I think we have a lot to talk about,"

Opal interjects. "From the looks of her, we need to get Lindsey back on her feet."

"Yes, let's." Janice turns serious. "Spill it, Lindsey. Where are you with that dickhead Chad?"

"How do you know about Chad?" I ask.

"Oh, I know more than you think. Don't forget I have a whole team of hackers at my disposal and they are very good." I love how Janice talks like the company is hers as much as it is Michael's.

So, I spill the beans and get through as much of the story as I can without going nuclear. I'm embarrassed when I reveal that I didn't see the warning signs after not hearing from Luke McKenna. "Yes, I feel naïve." I admit. By the time I get to the hotel part of the story, I feel my face beginning to flush red with anger. "The asshole had the audacity to act as though seeing me there meant nothing." But I'm shaking when I tell about the events as they occurred outside the office. "I guess I should have been more diligent about taking care of the details of setting up my business. I thought I would get to it when I had time. The asshole knew the business name I was going to use, stole it by registering it in his name, created a website, and somehow convinced Luke that we were partners." Then, I can't help myself as I get to the part about Michael and a tear leaks out of the corner of my left eye. "He knows about me and Michael; says he will ruin the IPO if either of us does anything to stop him."

"But you two haven't really done anything. What can he do?" Janice asks.

"He can do enough." I look down at my drink, a little embarrassed to admit this in front of Opal, who has been listening intently. "He must have hired a paparazzi or something because, although we haven't really done anything, it sure looks like we have."

"He has pictures?" Now Janice is fuming. "That little prick. So why haven't you gone to Michael? He can help. He said he's been trying to get ahold of you all week, but you won't respond."

"You think this business with Chad would be enough to keep me locked in my apartment for days, wishing the whole world would go away?" I pause and look up just in time to catch a glimpse of her coming in the door, headed to the counter, and I have to blink twice to make sure I am not imagining her. "Because I saw him, locked arm and arm with her, heading up the elevator to their hotel room."

"Who?" Janice asks incredulous.

"Her." I nod my head at her as she crosses behind Janice.

Janice turns to see who it is. "Julie?" She says way too loud, and crap... Julie heard her.

"Janice?" Julie, dressed in every day super model attire, smiles and puts her phone in her purse.

"You're just in time, sweetie," Opal interrupts, stands to greet her and shakes her hand. "Would you like to join us for a little girl time?"

Julie appears to be captured or confused by Opal's overture and pauses before she responds. "I'd love to." As she takes the fourth chair at the table, directly in my line of sight, she finally notices that I am there. "Lindsey, nice to see you again."

I have nothing to say to her, but being with Opal always somehow reminds me to mind my manners. The best I can come up with as a response is, "You don't have any coffee."

Opal raises her arm and waves to the front counter. "That's right, dear, how rude of me. Let me take care of it." Chris immediately notices, waves and Opal turns back to the table to smile at each of us in turn. "Now then, we have a lot to talk about so let's get to it."

CHAPTER 18

Michael

I AM ABOUT to give up my search, so I plop down in Janice's empty chair. Where the hell is she? She never leaves me alone for this long. Just where the hell is everybody? I know it's Friday but this is ridiculous. Of course Lindsey is gone, but I still wander past her desk with some senseless fantasy that she will be there and at least I can see her. And then that relentless suck up Chad hasn't even been at his desk. It's as though I've stumbled into some alternative reality and the plot twist hasn't been revealed to me yet. *Ah hah, Michael, jokes on you! In this reality you are the janitor and your shift's about to start. Go get your coveralls on and get busy cleanin', bucko.*

That's it. I'm going to HR. I'm telling on somebody.

As I reach the office of the head of our human resources department, I am thrilled and relieved as I get to her door and realize she is there, sitting at her desk. "Jordan!" I blurt out.

"What?" I obviously startled her, and she looks around as though someone is about to attack.

"You're here."

"Yes?" Now she looks really confused. "Am I not supposed to be?"

"Of course you are, thank God. But where is everybody else? Do you know where Janice is?"

"Usually attached to your hip. If she's not there, I don't know where she is."

"She's not in the office." Now that I'm sure I'm in the correct reality, I try to rescue my usual casual demeanor by sitting in a chair and kicking up my feet. "Did she ask for the day off?"

"Janice?" She looks at me in wonder. And I realize my stupidity. Like Janice would ever do such a thing. "The Janice? She doesn't ask… for anything. I'm more afraid of her than I am of you."

"Smart." I nod. "Okay, so you haven't heard from her?"

"No," she says.

"And where is Chad? I haven't seen him at his desk in days."

"He quit. Didn't you read my email?" She raises her eyebrow at me because she already knows the answer.

"He quit? Did he say why?"

"Chad? Did Chad say why?" She shoots me the 'here we go again, are you serious' look. "Of course he did. He quit to start his own business, wouldn't stop talking about it. Apparently he locked down some big contract and left without notice."

"Thanks. I need Alan. He here?" I ask.

"Michael?" She looks at me exasperated and starts to say something that I interrupt.

"Never mind, I'll check myself."

I buzz by Alan's desk but don't stop on my way to my office, and thankfully he's there. "Alan, my office and bring your laptop," I shout.

By the time I sit in my chair and look up, he is there. Alan never looks stressed, in spite of whatever my chaos level is. It kind of pisses me off that he can remain so calm no matter what I ask of him. I guess he's evolved and adapted defenses against me. I may have to up my game. "What's up?" He asks and sits in one of the chairs in front of my desk.

"I… " Over his shoulder and outside my open door I spot Janice. "Hold on. Where the heck have you been?" I yell just loud enough for her to hear me.

She takes her time placing her jacket and her purse in their appropriate places, in no rush of course, then joins us in my office. "I've been taking care of some things," she says as she situates herself in the chair next to Alan.

"Did you know Chad quit?" I ask her.

"Yes. Of course."

"Do you know that he left to start his own business?"

She looks down and straightens her skirt. "I may have heard something about it."

I can't believe that she is acting so casual. "Doesn't that sound a little more than coincidental seeing as how Lindsey just did the same thing... and he's been mucking around in her computer."

"She's not too happy about it," Janice responds.

"You've heard from her?"

"Of course," she says again and now I'm pissed.

I throw my hands in the air. "She hasn't returned my calls or texts all week."

"Michael." And I know I'm in trouble. She has the look as though she's the principal and I'm the kid who's been sent to her office for disciplining. "You were heading up a hotel elevator locked arm and arm with Julie."

"How do you know..." I don't even have to finish my question. "She saw us."

"Michael, you really do need to be more careful."

"You know I wouldn't do that. We were heading into a meeting about the IPO and... you know how Julie is, she never keeps her hands to herself."

Janice nods but maintains her grim demeanor. "This mess with Chad and now you, Michael, Lindsey is feeling a little... distraught... as you can imagine."

"Damn it." I begin to run through it in my mind,

how I get myself out of this, but first, "Alan. Have you been able to figure anything else out, as far as what Chad is doing?"

Alan shoots a confused glance at Janice. "Tell him," she says.

He types into his laptop and turns it to face me. "We know he spoofed her email and has been sending out messages, I just can't gain access to the content of the messages."

"Do we know who he has been communicating with?" I ask.

"Excel Ventures."

"That's Luke." And it hits me. "He's stealing her contract." I pull out my cell phone, zoom through my contacts, call Luke's cell and wait.

Voice mail. "Damn."

"Janice, what is Excel's main number?"

She rattles off the number as fast as I can enter it and I press send. "Excel Ventures, can I help you?" the receptionist asks.

I respond, "Luke McKenna, please."

"Oh, I'm sorry, he's just heading into a meeting."

"Who am I talking to?" I ask.

"This is Laura."

"Laura, this is Michael Sinclair."

"Oh, hello, Mr. Sinclair. Sorry, but Luke just stepped into a meeting."

"With who?" I ask.

"Chad Dixon of Superior Events and Occasions. It

shouldn't take long; I think they are just signing contracts. Should I have Luke call you back?"

I hang up before answering. "Let's go, Alan, bring your laptop." I am not letting that little shit get away with screwing over Lindsey, even if she does hate me.

"I might as well catch a ride with you two," Janice says and grabs her coat and purse. "This should be fun."

CHAPTER 19

Lindsey

DAMN, it's cold outside and if I didn't have so much adrenaline pumping through my body, I'd probably care. If I can pull this off and Chad falls for my plan this will be the greatest day of my life. I can't believe the little weasel is late for his own meeting. I glance toward the building with the hope that he is late and I didn't miss him, then I turn back toward the parking lot and there he is, heading directly toward me.

"Did you come to congratulate me on my big date?" He is looking as confident as ever.

"Chad."

"Or do you need a job still, because I will be hiring soon."

"Chad, I'm here with an offer and the hope that you will do the right thing." I pull out the contract that the lawyer worked overtime last night to prepare.

He ignores the papers. "I don't have time for this, Lindsey, I'm late," he says and starts to walk past me.

"Chad, I am trying to give you the opportunity to do the honorable thing. This is a purchase agreement. I am offering to buy you out."

He turns back to face me. "Why would I do that?" he asks.

"I'm hoping you're a not a bad person who wants to get his start this way. What if anybody finds out and your clients realize what you did? Do you really think they will want to continue doing business with you?"

He steps closer and points his finger in my face. "I warned you. Don't test me."

"Somebody else could find out, Chad."

"For your sake and your boyfriend's sake, you better hope that never happens."

"Please, Chad."

He swipes the papers out of my hand. "What is your offer?" he asks. "The purchase amount is blank."

"Well, I wanted to talk to you first. I have $10,000.00 cash I can give you and, once I sign the contract with Excel, I can get a loan to pay you another $12,000.00. There is a promissory note in the back that guarantees I will pay you the $12,000.00. That should cover the hotel contract and your start up costs. You will have all your money back and you will have done the right thing."

"This is a pathetic offer." He throws the contract back at me. "And what makes you think I care about doing the damn right thing?"

"It's all I have," I say.

"Good-bye, Lindsey. I'm late." He turns and strides away.

"I tried to make it fair," I say quietly. "I knew you'd never go for it."

CHAPTER 20

Michael

I'VE NEVER SEEN Janice run but I have to say I am impressed; she isn't breathing nearly as hard as Alan after our sprint to the offices of Excel Ventures. I turned what is normally a twenty-minute drive into a fifteen-minute drive and we ran as fast as we could across the parking lot and into the building. "Hi, Laura, buzz us through," I yell as we burst through the doors.

"Hello, Mr. Sinclair." She jumps out of her chair, shocked with the sight of three maniacs running through her lobby. "Of course."

I call back to her, "They in the main conference room?"

"Yes," she responds.

Thankfully, the main conference room is on the main floor, and I've been there many times, so I know right where it is. With Janice hot on my heels and Alan lagging a couple meters behind, laptop still open, we slam aside the two giant mahogany doors to the main conference room. "Hold everything," I yell, feeling like I'm in a movie.

Luke McKenna, seated next to Julie and across from Chad, looks up at me in total confusion. "Michael. What's going on?"

"You don't want to do this, Luke," I start.

"Michael, I think it's you who doesn't want to do this," Chad interrupts.

"Want to do what?" Luke asks.

"Sign a deal with this guy." I point at Chad.

Chad stands up and raises his arms to try to assure Luke. "It's okay, Luke, we used to work together, and I think Michael and I may have a misunderstanding. If you wouldn't mind giving us a moment, we can straighten this out easily."

Julie stands and grabs Luke by the arm. "It's okay, Luke, let's give them the room for a minute." He follows her out the door with a confused look still plastered to his face.

As soon as the doors close, I turn to Chad. "Did you really think you could get away with this?" I ask.

"Get away with what, Michael? Signing contracts for my new business?" He lifts a stack of papers off the table. "It's done."

"Do you really think they will still want to do business with you once we tell them what you did?" I ask. "We know you've been in her computer. We know you hacked her computer, spoofed her email and send fraudulent messages. That is a federal crime, Chad, you could go to prison."

"I doubt you can prove anything, Michael."

Alan interrupts and raises his laptop as though it is evidence. "That's where you're wrong, Chad. We can prove it."

"Who cares? So I did it. Only Michael here won't do a damn thing about it, but what he will do is have you two follow him out of here, quietly, and never say another thing about this."

"What makes you think I would ever do something like that?" I have to ask.

"You see, even though it appears you haven't talked to your girlfriend, I have." He pauses and a knowing smile spreads across his face. "You haven't spoken to her, have you? Oh, how sad for her. Did she lose her business and her boyfriend in the same week?"

Right about now I am getting just pissed enough to wrap my hands right around his pencil neck but I don't. Not yet. "You're dumber than I thought if you think I would let you get away with doing anything to Lindsey."

"Oh, not just her, Michael." He looks me straight in the eyes for the first time ever. "To you too. I am quite prepared to ruin your little IPO when I go public with your communication trail as you hunted her down then fucked her on that beach in Hawaii."

That one caught me by surprise. "Bullshit." Is all I can say.

"No, not really. I have a great snap of it." He lifts his phone. "She does have nice big tits. If you're into that sort of thing."

"I'm going to fucking kill you." I start to circle the conference table.

Janice grabs me so hard her nails dig into my arms to stop me. "Just hold on a second, tiger," she whispers calmly then calls to Alan. "Alan?"

Alan looks at Chad and smiles. "No you don't, Chad."

"Don't what, Alan?"

"Don't have the communications or the pic." He points to Chad's phone. "Open it up and look."

Chad enters the passcode to his phone and begins his search. "We'll see." He swipes, slowly at first, then at a frantic pace while his desperation grows and a pale flood moves down his drooping face.

"Let me save you the time, Chad." Alan is gloating a little bit now. "It's not backed up in your cloud storage either. You see I'm a much better hacker than you are."

"That's illegal," Chad squeals.

Janice answers this time. "Prove it."

"It doesn't matter, the contract is signed. If they try to back out of it, I will sue." He's nearly in tears as the doors swing open and Lindsey enters the room followed by two men in dark suits. Luke and Julie follow close behind.

"It will matter, Chad, if you're in jail and can't fulfill the contract." She turns to the two men who followed her and points to Chad. "He's all yours, gentlemen."

"You can't prove anything; hold on, guys, I was framed and set up by this hacker." Chad starts to back up toward the window.

Julie points to cameras in the corner of the conference room. "We recorded your confession from the next room. Agent Sparks and Agent Timmons watched the whole conversation with Lindsey."

I am speechless as I watch the larger of the two men circle one direction around the table toward Chad as the second heads the other way. "I'm Agent Sparks with the FBI," he says as he flashes his badge. "You're under arrest for electronic mail and wire fraud, Mr. Dixon. Place your hands behind your back." As the second agent reaches him, he pushes Chad to bend over the table and places handcuffs around his wrists.

When Chad rises, his face is covered in tears and he is blubbering as they lead him to the door. "Lindsey, please don't do this. I'm sorry. I didn't mean it. I'll sell you the company, just let me sign the documents we talked about and it's yours. Please don't press charges."

Lindsey crosses her arms and appears to contemplate her answer thoroughly. "Can we do that, gentlemen?" Lindsey asks the FBI agents.

"It's your decision," Agent Timmons responds. "You

can press charges or tell us you refuse and we let him go."

"You don't sign the contracts, Chad, and I'm sending you to prison." Lindsey pulls out a stack of papers from her bag, removes some pages, places the rest on the table, writes something on the first page then flips to the last page and signs her name. "Sign."

Agent Timmons releases Chad from one side of the cuffs and he takes the pen from Lindsey. "One dollar? And what about the promissory note? That is not what we agreed on."

"You refused that offer. This is my new offer, take it or leave it. "Lindsey hovers over Chad and sneers.

"But I have $20,000.00 in the hotel contract alone," Chad whines.

"Not my problem." Lindsey shakes her head and raises a single eyebrow. "Take it or leave it, that is my final offer."

Chad signs the paper and Lindsey slams a single dollar bill on the table next to him. "You are all my witnesses. Paid in full, now get the hell out of here."

Agent Timmons releases Chad from the second cuff, stares down at him and growls, "I suggest you stay very far away from these people and the FBI, Mr. Dixon."

Chad can't get out the door fast enough, and I am completely stunned. What the hell just happened here? I turn to Lindsey and she raises her hand to stop me. "One second," she says.

A moment later, Laura rings in to the speakerphone on the conference room table. "Okay, he's gone, guys." And the room erupts in high-fives and laughter. I back up to stand next to Luke, who looks as confused as I am.

"What the hell just happened here?" I ask him.

"Hell if I know." He shrugs.

"Somebody want to tell me what is going on here?" I plead over the cheers.

Lindsey walks toward me. "There's my hero, ready to kill poor Chad to protect me. I must say that was the most fun I've had in quite a long time."

I am stumped. "What are you talking about? Are you trying to tell me you planned all this out?"

"Well I—" she starts.

Janice and Julie interrupt. "We."

"Sorry, ladies. We… came up with operation 'Screw the Weasel' and thanks to a lot of help from Alan, pulled it off without a hitch."

"Alan?" He is currently trying to skulk out of my line of sight to escape my wrath. "You knew about this and didn't tell me?"

"Sorry, boss, but I'm more afraid of them than you." He shrugs.

Janice comes to his defense. "We needed you to put on a good show. We needed you in full protective mode which, by the way, I said would work and Lindsey said would not."

Julie moves to stand next to Lindsey. "Let's not forget about Opal."

"Of course not." Lindsey wraps her arm around Julie and Julie reciprocates. "She brought us all together and told us the importance of us girls working together. She's so delightful isn't she?"

"She is." Julie nods.

"Yes, delightful," Janice adds as she moves up to Julie's other side to join the full girl embrace.

I'm still confused. "How did you get the FBI to agree to help?"

"I can answer that one," Luke jumps in. "These knuckleheads are certainly not FBI; they work for me. You definitely should have let me in on it. I almost outed you guys."

"We knew you'd figure it out, boss. We had faith in you." The grinning employee also known as Agent Sparks turns to Julie. "That was fun though, thanks, Julie. You mind if we take off?"

"You guys are good to go. Thanks so much for your help," Julie replies.

"I will need my handcuffs though," Janice interjects with an ornery smile. "Thanks, boys."

I am still majorly confused. "Lindsey, I thought…" I point to Julie. "You thought that me… and Julie…"

"I did, for a minute. But Opal helped straighten me out, and Julie explained why you actually were at the hotel together."

"My bad, Michael." Julie rubs up and down on Lindsey's shoulder. "You know how I have a hard time keeping my hands to myself."

"That was a really good plan." I nod in appreciation. "You guys still could have told me. I *can* act you know."

"Oh look, he's hurt. Girls, we've hurt his feelings." Lindsey moves in and wraps her arms around me while the other two surround us in a group hug.

"You better kiss him before I do," Julie tells Lindsey.

"Oh you wish." She rushes to move her lips to mine and kisses me deeply. "My hero," she sighs.

"Our hero," Janice and Julie say in unison and plant a kiss on each cheek.

"Y'all are nutty." I'm still in shock that they pulled this off but what the hell. "I say we all go celebrate," I suggest.

"Yes, let's," they all answer in unison.

"Somebody grab the FBI before they get too far." I figure there is no reason why they shouldn't get to join the celebration.

"I'll get 'em." Luke jogs out the door.

Janice leads the rest of the pack, but I lag behind and Lindsey grabs my hand to pull me along. "Ahhh." She pulls me to her side and wraps my arm around her waist as we walk. "C'mon, you'll be okay, I promise."

"I still say I could have pulled it off." I put my head down and fake a sniffle.

She puts her arm around my waist and pats me on my ass. "Of course you could have, sweetie."

CHAPTER 21

*M*ichael

MULLIGAN'S IS a local Irish pub that I love, so we all decide to meet there. I'm not sure if it's true but the rumor around town is that the original owner went to a pub in Ireland and loved it so much that he bought it, had the interior entirely disassembled, then shipped to the U.S. so the exact feel of the pub could be recreated. It's probably not true; I think that same rumor is spread about every Irish pub in the U.S., but it sounds good, and the place really does feel like you've just stepped into a pub in a small town just off the Ring of Kerry. Huge wooden beams, stained so dark they almost look black, span the ceiling and match the wood covered walls. The stain is almost Guinness dark, like they mixed the beer with the smoke from your grandfather's pipe, and infused it into the wood. The aroma invites you in and says 'welcome, let's have a pint and tell some tales'. On any given night, random musicians seem to appear out of nowhere, and before you know it, a drumbeat slowly and quietly builds momentum just in time to be joined by any number of guitars. It doesn't take long, as long as the beer is flowing, before everybody is Irish and they all join together in song. And it always seems like the Irish are celebrating something. Tonight, it's Lindsey's victory.

Alan and I are at the bar waiting the obligatory ten minutes for a 'good pour' and the place is beginning to fill up. I could see right away when we arrived, that I would need to stay sober so that I could drive. Somebody has to. "So tell me how you did it, Alan," I yell because it's starting to get loud in here.

"Do what?" He smirks.

"You know what. How'd you hack him?"

"I can't tell you that, boss. A hacker's got to keep some secrets." He grabs the first finished beer, takes a sip, and has to wipe the foam from his lip. "Besides, if I tell you everything, you may feel like you don't have to keep me around anymore."

"You know that's not going to happen." I grab the other three beers and turn to head back to the table when it dawns on me. "And the picture?"

He stops and drops his head. "I was hoping you'd just forget about that."

"Really?" I know he didn't actually think I would forget.

"Gone… for good. I promise, boss." He says it and I believe him. "And I promise I didn't even look."

"We're going to pretend that's true." I put my shoulder into him to move him in the direction of our table. "And never talk about it again."

The beers barely touch the table before Janice is raising hers for a toast. I grab the remains of my one and only beer and raise my glass. "To the long-lasting success of Superior Events and Occasions." Janice pushes in, what I think is her fourth beer. It's a good thing she doesn't work tomorrow. "I'll be sending you a list of our upcoming events," she continues. "I expect a very good discount."

"Here, here," I add.

Lindsey drinks the last of her beer. "And on that note, I have a surprise for Michael so we are taking off."

"Awwhhhh." A collective sad note rings across the group.

"Thank you all so much for everything you did. I love you guys." She grabs my hand. "Stay and enjoy the night, food and drinks are on Michael."

"What?" I feign concern.

"You'll be okay." She winks at me because she knows I'm kidding. "Nobody drives home tonight. There is a car and a driver outside to drive you home when you are ready. No hurry, he's ours for the night."

As we turn and head toward the door, I hear Julie say, "That calls for another round." And a cheer erupts.

Lindsey attaches herself to my arm while we cross the parking lot, and I can't quite tell if she is just cozying up or using me as a stabilizer so she doesn't zigzag walk on the way to my car. I didn't really pay attention to how much she drank so it could be either... or both. The stillness of the night has brought with it a biting chill that wasn't there when we arrived at the bar, feels like a storm is coming. Our breath clouds in front of our faces as we walk. And then I realize I have no idea where we are going or what we are doing. "You have a surprise for me?"

She pulls on my side to get my ear closer to her mouth and whispers a breathy, "Yep."

"How much did you have to drink?" I ask.

"Not that much. Just the perfect amount actually."

Our cars are parked next to each other, and even if she thinks she has not had that much to drink, it is too much to drive. "Whatever you have spinning in that head of yours, you're not driving. I'll be taking you home," I say.

"Well, duh." She steps aside while I open the passenger door for her. "That's where your surprise is."

By the time we are standing in front of the elevator, waiting for it to arrive at the lobby and carry us up to her apartment, my head is whirring in confusion. What is this damn surprise? Why would she get me a surprise when she thought I had cheated on her? When did she have time, with everything else going on? The doors open, we enter the elevator and we both turn to face the opening after she pushes the number for her floor. I already have the instinctive habit of reaching for her when we stand next to each other, so I reach to hold her hand but she pulls back.

"Uh, uh." She shakes her head and takes a side step away from me. Then she raises both hands and gestures wildly around the interior of the elevator. "You might break it… no touching."

"You did that, not me."

"Just keep your hands to yourself, buster." She gives me the full, two-handed, stop signal just in time for the ding and the door opening to her floor.

I follow several steps behind her, keeping my distance as she heads for her apartment door. She fumbles through an impossibly large ring of keys, finally makes a choice and inserts a key into her door lock but does a double take when she spots me out of the corner of her eye. "What are you doing?" she asks.

I had stopped halfway down the hall. "You said no touching."

She slowly walks toward me, staring me in the eyes the whole time and then grabs my hand to lead me to her apartment door. As we walk, she moves my hand to the small of her back, then onto her ass. "Oh, there's going to be touching."

By the time she opens her door and we cross over the threshold, she has probably only taken three steps with my hand on her ass but my cock is already fully hard.

She turns to close the door behind me and smashes me against it, slamming it shut. Before I have a chance to get my balance, she thrusts her mouth onto mine, her tongue is passionately greeting mine and her hips are pushing hard against me. No doubt she already knows how happy my body is to feel hers.

And I don't care.

I want her to feel how fully hard I am for her and I can't fucking wait any longer. My body's rage, my animal desire to have her is already boiling over. I spin her and press her against the door then thrust my hips into hers as I move my mouth to her neck. She arches her head back as I move down to her collarbone and drink in her scent as my lips search for the next space to explore. I reach my right arm behind her, cross her back, grab the right side of her ass and pull her harder into me. She pumps her body up and down a couple of times, grinding into me, before she moans and drives her arm between us. Her hand has found my cock through my pants and is stroking up and down. And I'm about to explode already, so I have to stop her. I want to cum in the worst of ways but not like this, not without her. So, I lower myself down, out of her reach and open her blouse, button by button.

I push the fabric of her top to the side of each breast to reveal a lace white bra. The front hook is easy to decipher and each section drops to the side upon the clip's release. And her beautiful breasts greet me with fully erect nipples begging me for attention. I circle her left nub with my tongue as I move to take the entirety of her nipple into my mouth. If the tip were any tighter I think it might burst and I can't help myself as I take it between my lips and flick it with my tongue.

She moans, grabs my hair to pull my head back, and kisses me deeply. Then she glides between the door and me, down to her knees. I close my eyes because the room is spinning as she frees my cock and takes the head into her mouth. She only slides me fully into her warm wet mouth twice before she knows my intensity and stops. She rises, strokes my cock one more time with her hand on the way up and says, "Follow me."

My hand is in hers as I follow her across her apartment into her room. She leaves me at the base of her bed and moves back to the front of the room to switch on a standing lamp in the corner. She looks back at me, over her shoulder and says, "Remember this?" Then she grabs the sides of her skirt and slides it, along with a white lace thong, to the floor. Bending straight-legged and bare ass in front of me, she lingers and looks back in question.

I could look at that beautiful shaved pussy peeking out from beneath that amazing ass forever. "Oh, I remember," I say.

She stands and walks back toward me with her top open, her breasts swaying with her stride. Nothing covers her bottom half but a shining silver chain around her hips that hangs down in the middle, following the contour of her belly, with a ruby pendant pointing the way.

Only she passes me by, stroking my cock once again as she passes, then lays on her back on the bed. The shiny silver chain around her hips and the red gem glow in the light of the lamp.

"Now come to me," she says.

She has no idea.

CHAPTER 22

Lindsey

Maybe I shouldn't have just left him standing there, but I couldn't help myself. Something about teasing him by lying in front of him three-quarters naked, ready for him, makes me even hotter. He has to stare at me from the foot of the bed while I watch him strip. And I know he can't look away. He's been ready to burst since we walked through my apartment door. I can feel it, and I can see it in his eyes. He's like a caged beast ready to break free and now I'm making it worse. And I love it. He is breathing hard now as he watches me, looking super hot with the front of his shirt untucked, his zipper down and his beautiful cock standing upright.

I am so fucking horny and giddy I can't help myself when he starts unbuttoning his shirt. "Yay," I blurt out.

"Yay?" He laughs as he finishes with his shirt.

"Sorry. You're stripping for me, it's kinda hot."

"Kinda?" He raises an eyebrow.

"Very." I turn onto my belly and put my head on my hands to watch. He has an amazing body: trim and very muscular but not overly so with great pecs and amazing shoulders.

"Okay." He stops and says, "For a guy, there is no elegant way to get the rest of this off so close your eyes.

"Aahh," I tease.

"Close 'em," he commands, which makes me even hotter, so I do.

I can hear the thump of shoes being kicked aside and the rustling of clothes being removed. Then I hear nothing but the barely perceptible pad of feet across the floor and he says, "Keep 'em closed."

Then I hear nothing for what seems like forever. I think he's behind me but I don't want to open my eyes. I can feel my heart in my chest beating louder now. I can't take it any longer. "Michael?" I ask.

"Don't interrupt me." He is behind me. "Do you have any idea what an amazing ass you have?"

I am so hot already I feel that I may be dripping wet. "I do?" I ask.

"Yes." He is climbing on the bed behind me and running his hands up the middle of my legs as he goes. His lips are on the back of my thighs. As his lips cross over my ass, the breath catches in my throat. So slow that it is painful, he gradually works his way across my ass, up the small of my back and then to my neck. By the time he gets to my ear, he is panting. He grabs both of my hands and stretches our arms out above our heads and puts his full weight onto me. Every inch of my skin tingles with the touch of his body to mine. His swollen cock is pressing in on the crack of my ass. He nibbles on the back of my neck and says, "You know how long I've been waiting for this?"

"I have an"—I almost get out my response but I am interrupted by my own groan as he presses harder into my ass. His cock slides further down the crevice—"idea." I squeeze his fingers in mine as I fucking love the feel of him.

"I get to take my time with you." He releases my hands and starts to push himself up. "And this time we won't be interrupted."

"Huh! What was that?" I fake a look at the door.

"Very funny," he says as he lightly swats my ass.

"Thought I heard something," I lie. I straighten my arms and put them down to my sides while I concentrate on the feeling of him massaging my ass with his hands.

He swats me again... and massages again. "Liar."

"I may just lay here forever if you keep doing that." I'm beginning to see that starting on my stomach was a genius idea. He's going to want to thoroughly cover both sides of me.

I giggle and arch my back. I can't help it if I'm naughty sometimes. It's in my nature. I reach up and back with my left hand to find and caress his balls and he groans at the touch. They feel super swollen and tight, so I have to ask, "My goodness, Michael. Have you not... you know... since the elevator?"

He struggles to get out a, "No", while I continue to run my fingers across the base of his testicles.

Then I think about it and release them. "Or the beach?" I ask.

"Listen, I've been a little busy. So, no. It's been awhile."

If that were me, I would have broken out my vibrator as soon as I got home, the poor man. "Are you going to be okay?" I have to have a little fun with this. "Am I going to be okay? Is it dangerous?"

He sighs at my silliness. "I'm fine."

"Should we call the President and alert the National Guard?"

Smack, he swats me again. "Stop."

"And batten down the hatches, Cap'n?"

Smack, a little harder this time. "Lindsey—"

"Duck and cover?"

"That's it." Smack, even harder this time then he flips me over.

And I'm giggling like a little girl by the time he grabs my arms and pins them over my head. "Just wanted to make sure no animals would be harmed in the making of this film."

"Just you," he says just before he kisses me passionately.

"Woof. Promises, promises." I push out a pouty lip. "You forgot the massage after the last swat by the way."

"Oh, I'll massage you alright." He moves to the top of my neck, and I turn my head to the side as he slowly works his way down. I think I'm going to like this.

He takes his time before he gets to my aching right nipple that's been awaiting the arrival of his lips. And he doesn't disappoint as he gently grips it in his lips and flicks the tip with his tongue. His pace quickens just as he slides a single finger between my wet folds. How did he sneak that arm down there without me noticing, a masterful touch that nearly has me exploding in passion?

He pushes his finger deep inside me, back and forth, and up and down then presses hard against the top of my opening while pushing his palm against my clit. And he begins a slow but steady rhythm that doesn't stop as he moves down to pepper my belly with kisses. As he crosses the threshold of my belly chain, I feel him stretch me wider as he thrusts in a second finger to heighten the intensity, and his pace quickens.

By the time his lips pass by my hipbones, my clit is throbbing in concert with the thrust of his hand, anticipating every touch. But his palm stops its pressure as he lowers himself further to take my clit in his mouth. The thrusting hand straightens and accelerates its tempo.

I arch my back to push my swollen nub into his mouth while he reaches behind me to grab my ass and lift me higher. He sucks me into his mouth and presses down with his tongue. He can tell I am ready to go over the edge so he thrusts his hand in and out, faster and faster, and flicks the top of my clit repeatedly with his tongue. I go over the edge in a flood of ecstasy. My insides pulse and contract so hard and for so long on his fingers, it feels like I may never stop. I hadn't even realized I'm groaning loudly and pounding the bed with each pulse. Then he releases my clit and I shudder as the tension in my core lessens.

I open my eyes and he is looking up at me like he owns me. And right now, he does and he knows it.

I move to the side, push him to roll onto his back, swing my leg across him and lift myself so I am over him, sitting on his belly. "You okay?" he asks with a grin like a Cheshire cat.

"Never better."

"Good. For a moment there I thought we would have to alert the National Guard."

"And how." I nod in agreement.

"Didn't you have a…" He pauses to catch his breath when I reach behind me and start stroking up and down the shaft of his cock. After a moment, he continues, "Mmm… a surprise for me?"

"Uh huh." I say as I squeeze harder and continue to stroke. I left a condom on my bed stand, so I reach for it, pause the stroking and tear it open. I reach behind my back with both hands and slide the condom onto his cock.

"Wow," he says. "Nice move. Is that the surprise? A talent show?"

"Nope," I respond as I move his cock to my opening and begin to slide down onto him. He feels fucking amazing inside me and I almost lose my breath as my heart leaps with each additional inch. I almost forget to say, "Surprise." But I manage to eke out the single word.

He closes his eyes and arches his head back. "Good God. Never thought I'd make it." He groans.

I begin to slowly raise myself up and down the length of him, but I don't want to rush it. Each round trip feels better than the last. He is breathing hard now but grits his teeth as I reach behind me and begin to caress his balls and I pump.

"Aaagh." He lets out a roar and pushes me off him. He is up and pacing around my bed in a flash.

I turn to lie on my back, and I am confused.

"Just hold on a gosh darn minute." He paces again but keeps his distance, breathing hard. "I have been waiting and waiting. Just hold on. Too fast." He paces some more then stops by my dresser and works to control his breath. "Look at you, you're fucking perfect." He grabs a pencil off my dresser. "Almost." He hands the pencil to me and moves back. "Here, put this where you normally have it, by your ear." I do what he asks and he stands and stares.

I'm lying there with a pencil over my ear, my silky white blouse spread apart revealing my breasts, my belly chain shining in the dim light of the distant lamp. And I guess that does it for him because he just stands and stares in silence.

Until I spread my legs open for him and run my hands to the inside of my thighs. That puts him over the edge.

He lets out another roar and is on the bed in a flash. He throws his left leg over my right leg, lifts my left leg to his shoulder and thrusts his bulging cock back inside me. I am engorged with his animal desire and my insides pulse each time he thrusts himself inside me. The bonus is his thigh pressing against me, so I press hard with my hips against his leg. Each time he presses into me, my clit grinds against his leg. Faster and faster, harder and harder, he thrusts and I grind until we both explode with pleasure.

As the movement of his throbbing cock begins to lessen, he rests his head against my leg. I reach for him and pull his sweating body down to mine. "That was very good for me," I say.

"Me too," he says and shifts most of his body to my side. "Did you batten down the hatches?"

"Me? Nah. I love to live dangerously."

"But you could have been hurt," he teases.

"You can hurt me like that anytime you want." I move his hand to cover my breast and I know he can feel my heart still pounding.

"I'm in love with you. You know that, right?" he says.

"I'm in love with you too, Michael." I turn to look him in the eyes. "Take good care of my heart."

He moves his hand to the top of my breast, slides it down over my nipple again and my pulse presses against his fingers. "You've got a deal."

EPILOGUE

*L*indsey

LAST NIGHT WAS AMAZING, and I should be exhausted but I couldn't sleep, too much adrenaline still pumping through my veins. The event went off without a hitch, and Luke is thrilled with how everything went. Everyone had a blast. Not bad for a new company's first venture. He's promised to send me the details of their events for the rest of the year. Already, between Luke and Michael, I have a busy year ahead of me and word is spreading. I have a schedule full of meetings with potential clients lined up for this week.

I may have to start hiring some help soon, wonder if Chad is still available. "Ha ha ha." I crack myself up.

"Hmmm?" Michael stirs in bed next to me when he hears me laughing.

I roll over and nudge him the rest of the way awake. "Get up, I can't sleep. Let's go for a walk and get some coffee.

"Noooo, I'm sleeping," he whines. "What time is it?"

Perfect opportunity to use his own line on him, the one he uses on me every time he wants me to get up and go hiking with him. "Daytime," I say. "Besides, it's a nice day. Let's get some fresh air and some coffee."

"Fine," he says as he rolls out of bed and heads to the bathroom. His place is being renovated so we mostly stay at my place, and he has grown quite comfortable here. I think my neighbor Penny likes him better than me already.

I roll out the opposite side and throw on some sweatpants and a sweater that I left at the foot of the bed. I glanced at my phone to check the temperature outside; forty degrees Fahrenheit and sunny. I better take a jacket.

Michael is moving half-speed and seems like he's having a harder time getting moving than he normally does.

He had a big night last night too.

By the time we brush our teeth and get out the door, the temperature has risen five degrees, so I wrap my jacket around my waist. I wrap my arm in his, snuggle up to his side and we make our way toward Get Perky. I feel like the luckiest girl alive. My business is doing well and the love of my life loves me back.

Michael steps ahead of me when we reach the building and he opens the door for me. I step inside and head for the counter to order our coffee. This is our routine, as it has become. He secures us a table and I get the coffee. I primarily work from home these days but when I'm not at home, I am at my second office, Get Perky. Needless to say they know me well.

Chris is already at the register with my order entered and the total shining in the display. "Morning, Lindsey."

"Morning, Chris." I insert my debit card into the chip reader. "Thanks."

"How did everything go last night?" he asks.

"Better than I could have possibly imagined." I flash my left hand so he can see my new ring.

"He proposed?"

"Yep." I nod. "Can you believe it?"

"Yes, I can. You two are perfect together." He hands me my receipt. "And you said yes?"

I shoot him a confused look.

"Sorry, stupid question." He smiles and shakes his head. "Congratulations. I'm so happy for you."

"Thanks, Chris."

"Go ahead and sit down, I'll bring your order out when it's ready."

I turn to head to the area where we usually sit and when I round the corner, I see that Michael is not alone. Opal has his hand in hers and is listening to him speak. "Am I interrupting?" I ask.

"Oh no, dear. Sit down, please." I sit down and she opens her other hand for me.

I put my hand in hers and instantly feel the tingling warmth that always follows an Opal embrace. I can't stop the smile spreading across my face and I look at Michael who has the same dopey smile. We can't help it… we love this woman. "How are you this morning?" I ask her.

"Oh I've had a wonderful day so far." She's wearing her purple outfit this morning but hasn't taken off her hat yet.

I glance down to see her matching gloves and purse are on the table next to her. "Aren't you going to have a coffee with us this morning?"

"Not this morning, dear. I just wanted to stop by and congratulate both of you on your wonderful night." She smiles at Michael and glances down at my ring. "Everything came together for you just like I knew it would. You worked hard, risked everything, battled fiercely and won. Now you are getting everything you deserve. Both of you, and I am so happy for you."

"Something tells me I couldn't have done it without you, Opal."

"Oh, of course you could have. You just needed the encouragement and a little push here and there, but everything you needed is right inside you, it always was." She turns to look Michael in the eye. "And you... I know you'll take good care of her."

"Yes, ma'am." He nods.

The jingle of the door opening catches my attention, and I look up to see Janice walking our way. "Janice." I yell and jump to my feet to grab her for a hug.

"Good morning, you." She hugs me back and then pulls out a chair so she can sit down. "And you too, Michael. No, don't bother to get up." She teases. "Opal, so lovely to see you."

"Janice, how nice to see you. I thought you might be here this morning."

Janice hooks her purse on the corner of the chair and sits down. "Well, this being their second home, I knew they'd show up this morning. I wanted to find out how everything went last night." She glances at my hand before I have a chance to hide it under the table. "I see she said yes."

"You told her before you told me." I sock Michael in the shoulder. "She always knows everything before me."

"Oh don't be mad, sweetie. I know everything before he knows it too."

"She's not lying." Michael shrugs. "I don't know how she does it."

"You all make such a wonderful family." Opal is beaming with pride.

"Well, you'll have to teach me how you do it," I say to Janice.

"Oh it's not hard, he's an open book. I don't think he has a deceitful bone in his body."

Michael shrugs again. "She's not lying."

"Tell us how the event went last night," Janice says.

"It went very well, better than I expected actually. I'm very happy and Luke is already lining me up for the rest of his events this year," I respond.

She wags her finger at me. "Well, don't forget, we're next and I expect a very good price."

Chris walks up beside Michael and sets our order on the table. "Here y'all go. Opal, did you want something?"

"Oh no, thank you, Chris dear, I'm not staying," Opal answers.

Chris turns to Janice. "And you, miss?" Then I swear, for the first time ever I see Chris blush. "Can I get you anything?"

Opal interrupts, "Chris, have you met Janice?" Opal reaches over and grabs Janice's hand.

Something between a grin and smile spreads across Janice's face and Chris is speechless. "We've never officially met," Janice interjects.

Opal reaches out and takes Chris's hand in her other hand. "Janice, this is Chris. He is a wonderful young man."

Chris clears his throat and tries to gather himself. He hasn't stopped staring at Janice. "Nice to meet you."

"And you." And Janice is blushing now too. Janice… of all people.

I don't know how could this be happening, but I feel I should help out. "She'll have a large vanilla latte with soy milk," I say to Chris.

"Right away." I think I notice a bead of sweat on his brow just before he turns and heads back to the counter.

Michael and I shoot a look of disbelief at each other and a grin spreads across his face. "You okay, Janice?" he asks.

She doesn't answer.

"Janice?" I reach over and shake her arm.

She looks bewilderedly at Michael and says, "Of course I'm okay." Then she straightens herself in her chair and grins at me. "Why wouldn't I be?"

"Well." Opal begins to rise and we all rise with her. "I really must be going. Lindsey and Michael, I'm so happy for both of you. Lindsey, you take good care of him. And Michael, don't forget to take good care of her." Opal points to Janice. "She is very important but needs looking after too."

"This one?" He points at Janice too.

"Yes, this one." Opal nods.

"Of course she does, and I will," Michael agrees.

"We will," I interrupt and put my arm around his waist.

"Janice, I'm sure our paths will cross again." Opal grabs her gloves and her purse.

"I hope they do." Janice smiles.

Opal turns and heads toward the door. An older

gentleman in a knee length overcoat opens the door for her then follows her out.

We all sit down just as Chris arrives with Janice's coffee. "Here you are, miss."

They lock eyes and hold each other's gaze as Janice takes the cup from him. "Thank you... Chris."

He has a cup of his own and raises it up. "A toast," he says. "To Michael and Lindsey."

"To Michael and Lindsey."

~ Did you miss the Walker Brothers series?
Read Crash and Burn...

When Chance Walker was a child, he wanted to be a rock-n-roll god. He went to law school instead. Now, to honor his mother's final wishes, he must go back and follow his dreams. One kiss from his new guitar instructor rocks his world, but she has secrets of her own. Can he convince her they're meant to be together, or will he crash and burn?

BOOKS BY AMANDA ADAMS

The Walker Brothers

Crash and Burn

Alone With You

Up All Night

Make Me Forget

Magical Matchmaker Series

Stealing Christmas (Magical Matchmaker, Book 1)

Billionaire's Obsession (Magical Matchmaker, Book 2)

Other Books

Claimed in Shadows (with Luna Davers)

Coming Soon from Amanda...

Sweet Mountain Mystery (Romance) Series

You can also find Amanda's books in German, French, Spanish and Italian.

ABOUT THE AUTHOR

JOIN Amanda's VIP Reader List!
http://bit.ly/AmandaNews

Amanda Adams writes funny, sexy, new adult and contemporary romance, as well as a new YA romantic cozy mystery series. A full time author, Amanda spends her days trying to walk more and type less. If she eats a salad for lunch, she makes sure to reward herself with chocolate after (as any reasonable woman would do.) Her books are free of cheating--with a guaranteed HEA. Enjoy!

Connect with Amanda:
Facebook: http://bit.ly/AmandaAFacebook
Twitter: @amandaadamsauth
www.amandaadamsauthor.com

www.ingramcontent.com/pod-product-compliance
Lightning Source LLC
LaVergne TN
LVHW011829060526
838200LV00053B/3947